Believe my Word

Believe my Word

Linda K. Hubalek

Butterfield Books Inc.

Lindsborg, Kansas

Believe my Word

Rancher's Word Series, Book 2

Published by Butterfield Books Inc.

Printed Book ISBN: 9798582404286

Library of Congress Control Number:

Printed in the United States of America.

This book is a work of fiction. Except for the history of Kansas mentioned in the book, the names, characters, places, and incidents either are the product of the author's imagination or are used fictitiously, and any resemblance to actual persons, living or dead, business establishments, events, or locales is entirely coincidental.

Retailers, Libraries, and Schools: Books are available at discount rates through Ingram and Amazon distributors.

To contact the author or the publisher *Butterfield Books Inc.,* please email to staff@butterfieldbooks.com or write to PO Box 407, Lindsborg, KS 67456.

Romance Books by Linda K. Hubalek

Brides with Grit Series

Rania Ropes a Rancher

Millie Marries a Marshal

Hilda Hogties a Horseman

Cora Captures a Cowboy

Sarah Snares a Soldier

Cate Corrals a Cattleman

Darcie Desires a Drover

Tina Tracks a Trail Boss

Lorna Loves a Lawyer

Helen Heals a Hotelier

Faye Favors a Foreman

Amy Admires an Amish Man

Grooms with Honor Series

Angus' Trust * *Fergus' Honor* * *Gabe's Pledge*

Mack's Care * *Cullen's Love* * *Seth's Promise*

Adolph's Choice * *Nolan's Vow* * *Elof's Mission*

Jasper's Wish * *Tully's Faith* * *Kiowa's Oath*

Mismatched Mail-Order Brides Series

The Peashooter Society's Plan

Amelia Changes her Fellow

Avalee Exchanges her Fiancé

*Maggie Shifts her Gent * Maisie Swaps her Groom*

Molly Switches her Man

*Nadine Trades her Partner * The Christmas Plan*

The Rancher's Word Series

Accept my Word

Believe my Word

Give my Word

Have my Word

Brenner Family

Here's a list of the family members who grew up on the Cross C Ranch.

Adoptive Grandparents: Isaac Connely and Kate Wilerson Connely *(Cate Corrals a Cattleman)*

Parents: Sarah Wilerson married Marcus Brenner *(Sarah Snares a Soldier)*

Adopted eight children in 1873:

Marty, married Lucy Smith *(The Christmas Plan)*

Maggie, married Peter Gehring, adopted Christian, Bonita, and Alice *(Maggie Shifts her Gent)*

Molly, married Tobin Billings, adopted Tim and Tom *(Molly Switches her Man)*

Maisie, married Squires Miller *(Maisie Swaps her Groom)*

Moses, married Faith Geller *(Accept my Word)*

Matthew, but goes by his middle name, Asher *(Have my Word)*

Mark, but goes by his middle name, Beckett *(Give my Word)*

Micah, but goes by his middle name, Carsten *(Believe my Word)*

Hamner Family

Parents: Oskar and Annalina Hamner

Leif Hamner, first wife, Britta, deceased.

Second wife, Tina Martin. *(Tina Tracks a Trail Boss)*

Children: Robby, Emma *(Believe my Word),* Oliver, Finn, Saul

Dagmar Hamner, married Cora Elison. (Cora captures a Cowboy)

Children: Nils, Theo, Pernilla, Sigrid, Abner, Baldwin, Ebba, Hadwig, Inga, Taddeus, Walt, Gottfrid

Rania Hamner, married Jacob Wilerson. *(Rania ropes a Rancher)*

Children: Alva *(Have my Word),* Harry, Felix, Juliana

Hilda Hamner, married Noah Wilerson. *(Hilda Hogties a Horseman)*

Children: Greta *(Give my Word),* Inga, Karin, Justina, Kirstin

Chapter 1

On the train, May 1893

"Oh, how I'd love to be there," Greta Wilerson mentioned to no one in particular as she read the newspaper while sitting at the dining car table.

The six of them, Carsten Brenner and his brothers Asher and Beckett, and the neighboring first cousins, Emma Hamner and Greta and Alva Wilerson, were on the train for the first leg of their trip to Texas. After boarding the train at Clear Creek, Kansas they had gone to the dining car to have breakfast since they left early this morning.

This trip was planned by their grandfathers, Isaac Connely and Oskar Hamner. The young women's grandfather, Mr. Hamner, wanted them to see the Texas Ferguson Ranch where the Hamner family emigrated from Sweden and then started their Texas cattle trail drives up to the Kansas railyards.

His grandfather, Isaac, suggested the brothers accompany the women for their safety and should also decide if they wanted to commit to ranching the family's Cross C Ranch for their career. Still, Carsten thought it was a matchmaking scheme.

"Where? What are you reading about?" Alva asked her cousin.

Greta folded the newspaper she was reading down to a quarter size to highlight the article and handed it to Alva.

"The Kentucky Derby at Churchill Downs in Louisville, Kentucky, is *this* Saturday, May 10th. Can you imagine being in that crowd to watch the famous horse race?" Greta's voice expressed excitement.

Carsten raised his eyebrows at his brother, Asher, sitting across the table from him. Asher shrugged, apparently not interested in a race in Kentucky. His other brother, Beckett, leaned forward with interest. They were triplets, all brown-haired and blue-eyed, originally named Matthew Asher, Mark Beckett, and Micah Carsten. Still, they all started using their middle names after their grade schoolteacher called them by A, B, and C to keep them separate from their five older siblings whose names also started with *M*. Not that their request made a difference to their mother, Sarah Brenner, or grandmother, Cate Connely. Either woman could rattle off their three names as one if they were in trouble or wanted all of their undivided attention at once.

Greta, the oldest daughter of Hilda and Noah Wilerson, would be interested in the famous horse race because she spent more time on horseback than the average girl. Her mother, Hilda, raced horses when she was younger, and the family still trained and sold horses for a living.

Beckett would rather spend time training young bucking horses than riding a tame horse to check the cattle herd. He and Greta had that in common. They both liked riding spirited horses; the faster, the better.

"Let me read that when you're done with it, Alva," Beckett asked.

"Wait, there's also an article about the Chicago World's Fair I want to read first. That's what I'd be interested in seeing," Alva said as she concentrated on the newspaper.

Now Asher looked interested in the conversation.

"It says the World's Columbian Exposition, also known as the Chicago World's Fair, celebrates the

400th anniversary of Christopher Columbus's arrival in the New World in 1492. The fair opened the first of May and doesn't close until October," Alva murmured as she continued to read.

Carsten turned back to watch Greta's mouth twist as her mind worked. The six of them had grown up together, going to the same country school, and he knew Greta was plotting something by her facial expression. The tall, blonde woman was a ball of energy and always planning something. Her cousin, Alva, was shorter, but had the Scandinavian's pale skin and blonde hair matching her cousin, because their mothers were twins.

"I know Grandpa wanted us to go on a trip together, but I'd prefer to go to Kentucky instead of Texas," Greta announced.

"You can't do that. Grandpa paid for our trip," Emma said.

Emma's comment made Carsten think how different she was from her cousins, who were only related because Emma's stepfather was a brother to the cousins' mothers. Emma was thoughtful, compassionate, and had always intrigued Carsten.

Emma matched her mother in appearance and size. Both were petite with brown eyes, which reminded Carsten of warm molasses. The only difference in their black hair was Tina's now had silver threads running through it.

"I've heard enough stories about our family's trips back and forth to Texas that I can imagine every creek and river they crossed," Greta announced. "He'd want us to see something that interests *us*. Therefore, I'm going to Kentucky instead of Texas. I can switch my ticket at the next stop and get on the train going east instead of switching to the southern line."

"No, Greta, you can't just decide to leave the group and travel alone," Emma gasped.

"I'll go with her," Beckett piped up.

Emma's eyes widened with surprise.

"This trip to Texas is important to our family, so we have to—" Emma emphatically stated, but Greta put up her hand palm out to stop her.

"I know it's important to you because of what happened to you and your family. You want to see where it all happened," Greta gently told Emma.

Emma was a toddler when she, her widowed mother, then Tina Martin, and her brother, Robby, were in a train wreck near Austin and were separated because Tina was pulled from the wreckage unconscious. The two siblings were placed in an orphanage until Leif Hamner united the family.

Tina was cared for in a saloon for a few days, where she gave birth to baby Oliver. A saloon employee was ordered to get rid of Tina's infant, and the baby was placed in the back of Leif's wagon, hoping the rancher's wife would take care of him. Leif tracked down the infant's birth mother and then Tina's other children in the orphanage.

The Martin family traveled with the Hamner family as they drove their last herd of Texas cattle to Ellsworth, Kansas. Leif and Tina married and settled near their siblings and parents.

"But I don't care to see it. The four of you can continue on your trip, though," Greta suggested, but Carsten noted Alva looked anxious about the trip now too.

"Why don't you want to go to Texas, Alva?" Asher asked.

"I'm guessing because of what Emma's uncle, Sid Narker, did to her mother," Greta offered.

Carsten watched Emma lower her head to hide her embarrassment, even though she'd never known her deceased uncle. But her uncle violated Rania Wilerson before she was married, producing her cousin, Alva. It was a known fact that it happened, but Jacob Wilerson married Rania and had been Alva's father since her birth.

"Greta, you didn't have to bring that up. That was twenty years ago," Alva scowled at her cousin.

Carsten watched the tension rise around the table. Would the cousins get along on this trip together, or not? They were close to each other, but this trip had already brought tensions to the surface.

Asher put his elbows on the table and looked across to Alva. "I'd love to explore the Chicago World's Fair with you, Alva. How about we go on our own too?"

"What! No, we're supposed to go—" was all Emma got out before Alva stuck her hand across the table to Asher.

"I accept your suggestion. I'd love to see the pavilions highlighting countries around the world instead of the Texas countryside. It can't look much different than Kansas'," Alva said as she waited for Asher's hand to clasp hers and shake on it.

"It's all right, Emma," Carsten tried to assure his friend, but his heart rate kicked up a notch, thinking about being on a trip alone with Emma. "I'll escort you to Texas and back."

Emma's gaze jerked up to meet his eyes. She stared at him a moment before her right eyebrow raised and she folded her arms across her chest.

"And why would you do that, Carsten? No one else wants to go to Texas," Emma tried to sound impassive, but Carsten knew she was upset in her quiet way.

"Besides promising our grandfathers I would do it?" Carsten knew that was the wrong thing to say when Emma's shoulders slumped, and he tried to backtrack to save her pride and his self-worth in her eyes.

"I understand how important this trip is to you, and I'd be honored to accompany you."

What he'd like to say—if they weren't sitting with a table full of relatives—is that he wanted to spend time alone with her. They all grew up together, but Emma caught his eye when she blossomed into adulthood. Unfortunately, his brother, Beckett, showed interest in Emma for a while, and Carsten didn't mention his interest in her after that. But it had been several months since Beckett escorted Emma to a social. This could be Carsten's opportunity to see if Emma had an interest in him.

Emma studied Carsten for a moment before turning to her cousins. "Do you think it's wise to split up as couples and go different directions? What would our parents think of us not staying together as a group?"

Greta's sly grin was typical of her impulsive life. "I've been waiting for a chance to explore life past our county for a long time. And to get the chance to see the famous race at Churchill Downs? *Fate* put me here the Saturday before the famous Kentucky Derby."

"You're as impulsive as your mother, Greta," Beckett said as he shook his head, but there was a gleam of appreciation in his eyes. Did Beckett like Greta instead of Emma?

"The train is slowing down and will be stopping soon. Let's get off, grab our luggage, and change our tickets to go to Kentucky," Beckett said as he took the cloth napkin off his lap and set it on the table.

"Beckett—" was all Carsten got out before Beckett put his hand on his shoulder and squeezed it. Beckett leaned close and whispered so the others could not hear him. *"You're* welcome to follow Emma anywhere you want because *I* won't."

Carsten stared at Beckett to be sure he understood what he thought Beckett meant.

Beckett's nod confirmed it. Carsten was free to pursue Emma if he so wished.

Beckett stood and walked around the table to Greta's chair. "You ready to start our adventure, Greta? Maybe we can tour some horse farms in Kentucky besides attending the races."

"Better keep a close watch on Greta, or she'll be riding in the Derby herself," Asher teased, knowing how Greta loved to race her horses.

"That would make me happy and Mama proud," Greta answered back as she stood up and took Beckett's arm.

"Wait," Carsten said before the couple left the car. "Should we meet back here where the trains converge before we travel back home? I think our grandfathers would expect that."

Beckett hesitated a moment but then answered. "Yes, I think that's a good idea. Shall we meet back here at this depot in ten days?"

"But what if our travel time changes since we're heading in different directions?" Asher asked.

"Ten days should be enough time, and if not, send a telegraph to this train depot, so we know if someone is delayed," Beckett answered with a shrug. He wasn't worried about the timeframe of traveling to Kentucky and back.

"Well, then, we'll see you in ten days," Greta said with excitement before she and Beckett quickly left the dining room.

Emma looked shocked when she turned back to the table. "Can you believe they are just taking off for Kentucky like that?"

"Knowing those two so well?" Asher sighed as he put his napkin on the table. "Yes. They are impulsive, but I think they'll have a grand trip."

Asher looked across the table at Alva and studied her a long moment before saying, "And I think we'd enjoy seeing Chicago and the World's Fair together, Alva. I was serious when I suggested it. Were you too when we shook hands, Alva?"

"I was joking, but it would be a once-in-a-lifetime experience," Alva told Asher, but she turned to Emma to address her next.

"But I'll continue on to Texas with you, Emma, if you want me to."

That was so like Alva to think of her cousin and give up her dream trip if Emma said she wanted her along.

"It might be easier if only Carsten and I go alone so that we might change our itinerary," Emma said as she looked sideways at Carsten.

"How so?" Alva pressed her cousin.

"Instead of spending time on the Ferguson Ranch as we'd planned, I'd like to go further south to San Antonio to find my father's grave, and then stop in Austin on the way home."

Alva nodded as she wrapped her hands around her cousin's arm. "I know you've always wondered about your father's death and the mystery surrounding it."

Emma nodded. "But I also want to see the orphanage in Austin where Robby and I spent time after the train accident, if the home still exists. I also feel it is important to visit the graves of Leif's first wife and son in the Austin cemetery too."

"Your stepfather would appreciate that," Asher added, to let Emma know he supported her change of plans.

"I'd like to accompany Emma on her mission, Asher. I don't mind if you and Alva head north while we travel south," Carsten said to smooth everyone's worry.

Asher held his hand out to Alva again, and she took it to shake while smiling in her serene way.

"Shall we explore Chicago and the World's Fair together, Alva? It's a unique opportunity we'll miss—unless we do it now."

"I accept your proposal, Asher," Alva said with a hint of excitement in her voice. Was that because of the adventure or because Alva would be spending time with his brother?

"Emma, I believe we need to change our train tickets too if we're traveling to San Antonio first," Carsten said as he stood and offered his arm to the petite woman.

"Thank you, Carsten. I appreciate your change of plans for me," Emma said quietly.

Carsten nodded, but he was thrilled by how the group was splitting up. He wanted to spend time alone with Emma, time without his brothers watching him. This was the perfect opportunity to decide if they belonged together on the ranch as husband and wife.

Chapter 2

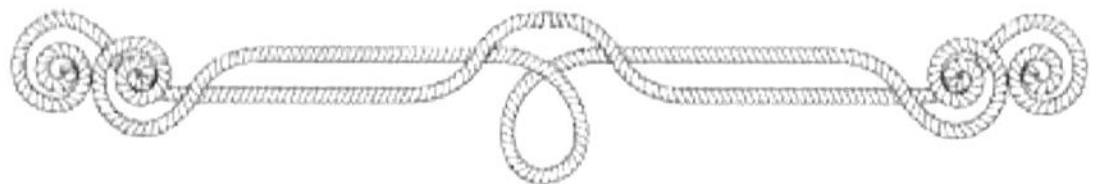

"I still can't believe they took off on their own," Emma muttered as she looked out the train car window after they boarded the southbound train.

The rest of their group was still waiting for their trains. Greta and Alva stood on the depot platform excitedly chatting about something while Asher and Beckett stood beside them, relaxed but attentive to the women.

Emma couldn't hear what they were saying, but she bet the cousins were glad to get away from her. Well, not Alva, but definitely Greta. Emma loved them both dearly, but silent frictions between their mothers sometimes interfered with the daughters.

It was a strange triangle of relationships with Alva trying not to play favorites. Alva and Greta were first cousins, but Alva was also Emma's first cousin because Emma's uncle assaulted Alva's mother, Rania.

"I can," Carsten said as he patted Emma's forearm. She wished Carsten would wrap his arm around her shoulders because she'd lean into him for support. Carsten was always so kind and polite to her.

"Greta is impulsive, and Beckett has always wanted to see a big racetrack like Churchill Downs. It was the perfect excuse to leave us," Carsten explained.

"And what about Alva and Asher?" Emma asked, but she already knew the answer to that question. Alva was sensitive to her origin, although she never said a word about it to Emma.

Now Carsten moved his arm to rest it on the back of the seat and squeezed her shoulders.

"Your uncle's actions never had anything to do with you, Emma. Honestly, I can see Asher and Alva touring *every* building at the fair, reading *every* plaque on *every* display, and thoroughly loving every minute. Can't you too?" Carsten challenged Emma.

Emma couldn't help but smile, thinking of the two exploring the exhibits.

"Yes, you pegged their matching delight for details perfectly. Thank you for reminding me that the differences between our cousins are alright."

"And normal. I'm glad to take a trip without my brothers," Carsten confessed.

Emma could understand that. The triplets had done everything together since birth.

Although the triplets tried to look different now in their different haircuts and clothing, they looked identical in their facial features. Carsten was last born and the smallest of the triplets at birth. But now, his slightly shorter stature was only noticeable when the three brothers stood together.

"Do you think your brothers feel the same way?"

Carsten thought about it a moment but then slowly nodded. "Yeah, although it will take Asher longer to realize it. He's always been in charge of the three of us, being the oldest."

The train car lurched as the train started to pull away from the depot. Emma looked out the window at the rest of their group waiting for their trains. Now Alva and Asher searched the windows for her and Carsten while Greta and Beckett happily conversed and ignored the activities around them.

Emma lifted her hand, and Alva saw her through the glass. Alva said something to Asher, and they both waved their farewell as they watched the train start to move.

Emma continued to watch out the window as the train slowly moved through town. Although she'd known Carsten all her life, it seemed strange to be alone with him now.

"Are you having second thoughts about our trip to Texas, Emma?" Carsten quietly asked, sincerely worried about her.

"No, I… Well, yes. We know each other, but is it proper to be traveling together?"

"I promise to be the perfect escort. A proper gentleman," Carsten answered. "Besides, you grew up with four brothers. I bet you know a few tricks to knock an unwanted admirer, or me, down. Maybe I should be worried about being alone with *you*," Carsten's mouth turned up on one side as he tried not to break out in a grin.

"Ha, ha, Carsten," Emma said as she turned to stare at him. "I'm glad it turned out this way when I think about it more. I prefer to travel alone with you instead of the group. It will be easier to decide what to see and do without six different opinions."

"As far as I'm concerned, you choose what you want to see and do, and I'll go along with it."

"Are you sure?"

"Yes, although I'll say no to robbing banks, getting drunk, or eating eggs."

"What? Don't you like eggs for breakfast? You didn't have any at breakfast this morning, now that I think about it."

"I gag thinking about a runny egg yolk," Carsten said as he shuddered a little to prove his point.

Emma smiled at Carsten, thinking about how she would enjoy this time with him. He was a good man, and she'd always admired him and was a little smitten with his charm too.

"All right. We'll stick with oatmeal and bacon for breakfast *and* stay out of saloons and banks. Deal?" Emma suggested, turning sideways in the seat to hold her hand for Carsten to shake on her suggestion.

"Deal," Carsten replied as he squeezed her hand and let go again.

"And to make you feel better traveling alone with me, I ran across the street to a jewelry store after I exchanged our tickets," Carsten said as he reached into his vest pocket and pulled out a ring. "Want to wear this ring while we're traveling so it looks like we're married?"

"You bought me a *wedding ring*?" Emma gasped as he dropped it into her palm.

"Consider it a souvenir ring to remember our trip. Will it pass for the real thing though?"

It was a delicate gold band featuring a large center diamond surrounded by a circle of smaller diamonds. Was the ring gold plated, or solid gold? Real diamonds or fake stones? Emma couldn't ask since it was a gift but she loved it no matter what materials it was made out of.

"Oh yes," Emma said as she pulled off her left glove and slid it on her ring finger. "You guessed about right on the size too."

Emma held up her spread fingers to admire the ring and Carsten grasped her hand, bringing it up to his lips and kissing the ring.

"I'm glad I was impulsive and bought the ring for you then," Carsten said as he let go of her hand.

Emma missed the warmth of his hand as soon as he let go of her hand but still felt safe and comfortable sitting beside him. She realized there wasn't another man she'd want to spend time with other than Carsten Brenner.

Chapter 3

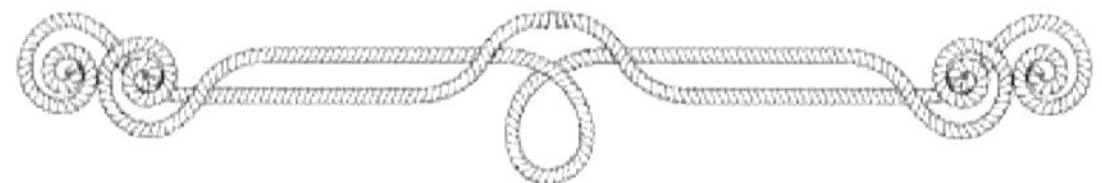

"Could you tell me where the city cemetery is located, sir?" Carsten asked the depot agent after he and Emma had departed the train at San Antonio and collected their baggage.

"Which cemetery are you looking for? There are about thirty in the city limits," the middle-aged man said as he leaned forward to hear above the noise of the crowd of people in the packed depot. They had waited in line several minutes before they could ask the question.

Carsten looked at Emma, but her shoulders slumped, apparently not knowing the answer.

"Uh, I'm not sure what cemetery, but the burial would have been twenty years ago," Carsten supplied a hint to the man.

"That narrows it down to about five cemeteries then. Any chance the person could be a Catholic, Lutheran, or Masonic? That would help your search."

"Emma?" Carsten asked her in hopes of giving the man more information.

"Um, we're looking for my father, who was killed in 1873. My mother never mentioned a church they may have attended," Emma told the agent.

"That eliminates the old city cemetery then. It was full in the 1850s, except the Masonic and Odd Fellows adding on to it later. Your best bet is to head up to Powder House Hill on the east side of town."

"All right. Which direction do we walk in?"

"Best to walk south down the block and catch an electric streetcar. Ask for more directions when you get there," the man said before looking behind them and calling out, "next person, please."

Carsten gently grasped Emma's elbow and moved her out of the way of the impatient man behind them, waiting to ask his question next.

"Let's return our bags to the baggage room for safekeeping and go find out," Carsten said as he hefted both their bags and pointed to the opposite end of the depot.

"I'm beginning to doubt whether we can wander through five cemeteries, find my father's grave, and get back on the train tonight, though," Emma said as she followed Carsten.

"It's hard to say, but at least we won't have to carry our bags along all day if we check them in now."

Carsten noticed Emma bit her lower lip, a habit she did when she was worried about something.

"Did you not want to leave your bag, or are you worried about the streetcar?" Carsten asked before they reached the other door.

"No, neither. It's just… I didn't think San Antonio would be so big. What if we can't find his grave?" Emma asked.

Carsten hated to admit she had a valid point. Martin could be a common name in this big city.

"Then we visit the courthouse for the death record. Churches in the area would have records of the burial also."

"Of course. I'm sure the crime was featured in the newspaper at the time too. We can find which cemetery my father was buried in," Emma said with renewed determination.

"Do you know anything about the school where he taught? The school name or the street would be helpful."

Emma sighed and twisted the drawstrings of her reticule around in her fingers.

"No, I don't. Since I hadn't planned to go to San Antonio, I didn't ask my mother for locations and details."

Carsten looked around as he tried to think, not wanting Emma to see his insecurity. This big city was as foreign to him as Emma, but she counted on him to lead. What would his father, Marcus, do in this situation? He'd say stop, if you can, and take stock of the problem before planning your next move.

"Let's go to the right area and see what we can find," Carsten suggested as he touched Emma's lower back to guide her toward the exit of the depot.

"Good idea, Carsten," Emma smiled up at him, making him feel appreciated by the woman. He could get used to exchanging looks with this beautiful woman. But could she like him as more than a friend? Possibly spend the next fifty years together? This trip would be a good way to find out. Now he was glad that Greta read the newspaper and spoke up about going to Kentucky. Who knew Greta's impulsive behavior would help him out?

*

"Do you know the name and date of death?" the church sexton asked at the third cemetery Carsten and Emma walked to this afternoon. The middle-aged man was trimming the shrub bordering the front of the church's cemetery and put down his clippers to visit with them.

"Robert Martin. Died March 17, 1873," Emma said, getting used to providing the information needed.

"Do you know if the grave has a headstone or wooden cross to mark it?"

"The school board paid for a stone to be placed on the grave."

"The school board? Why would they do that?" The man turned quickly to study Emma.

"My father was a schoolteacher who was murdered in his classroom. The school board took care of the funeral and expenses," Emma replied, her chin rising as her face blushed. She was getting flustered, having to explain the details of her father's death at every cemetery they visited.

Carsten put a hand on Emma's lower back to show his support, and he felt her relax against it.

"Ah, the schoolhouse shootings. I was a young married man when that happened. Yes, I do know where those graves are," The older man's eyes lit up as he tapped his index finger against his temple. "I don't have to look it up. They are in Section F. Go up the drive until you see the section letter. Proceed until you see the large Wilson tombstone and then turn right down that side lane. It should be on the right, about halfway down that lane. Look for a mound of dirt next to the old Martin grave. That grave hasn't settled yet."

"Thank you, sir. I can't tell you how much this means to me," Emma replied as she reached to shake the man's hand.

A new grave next to the old one? Something bothered Carsten about that.

"You said a new grave. Was it a relative of Robert Martin?" Carsten asked, causing Emma to look up at him with confusion in her eyes.

"Doubt it. It was Rachael Jarvis. Young woman who died about four, five months ago."

Emma's eyes widened with surprise because Jarvis was the name of the man who shot her father.

"Who was her husband?" Carsten asked, knowing Emma was too stunned to ask.

"Simon Jarvis. He works at the newspaper up the street," the man pointed to the north, and Carsten could see the two-story brick building they had passed by when walking to the cemetery.

“Thank you for the information, sir. We'll walk up to the graves now,” Carsten said as he shook the man's hand to thank him.

“Glad I could help,” the man said as he picked up his clippers again and returned to his work.

“Carsten, why do you think the man thought it possible this Mrs. Jarvis was related to my father?” Emma asked, holding on to Carsten's elbow as they followed the gravel lane into the cemetery.

“No clue, but we can find out when we visit Simon Jarvis next,” Carsten stated as he pointed to the Wilson tombstone.

“This is where we veer to the right.”

“And there's a newer grave,” Emma said as she stopped and stared at the mound in the near distance.

Emma was about to see where her father was buried, and it affected her.

“Come on. I'm with you. Let's go pay our respects to your father,” Carsten urged her.

“I don't remember Robert Martin, Carsten. Leif has always been my father in my mind. But now I feel...”

"What, Emma?" Carsten patiently waited by her side until she decided to walk to the small gray flat stone he could now see by the newer grave.

"Sad? Afraid? A deranged man killed my father. I can't fathom the horror my mother felt as she walked into the school and saw her husband on the floor, his blood from his chest wound spreading across his shirt."

Carsten pulled Emma against his chest to hold her close, wishing he could wipe that image from her mind.

"And then have the murderer shoot himself in the head after explaining to my mother he did it because my father had an affair with his wife?" Emma whispered as she trembled in Carsten's arms.

"The man had to be out of his mind, confused by something that set off a terrible string of actions," Carsten said to console Emma. "Do you want to see his grave, or turn away, Emma? Either way, I'm right beside you."

Emma pulled away from Carsten's arms and drew a deep breath.

"I want to stand at his grave, Carsten. I need to see where he was laid to rest."

Emma reached Carsten's hand and laced her fingers with his before walking forward to stand in front of her father's headstone.

"Robert Martin, 1845 1873" was all that was carved in the small gray stone. Robert was only twenty-eight years old, leaving behind a pregnant wife and two young children.

Emma's gasp pulled Carsten away from his thoughts.

"My father is buried next to George Jarvis and his wife, Maria, who George killed before going to the schoolhouse," Emma said as she pointed to the gravestones on the left side of her father's stone. Carsten's mind had been on the Martin grave and the new grave to the right of it.

"I guess if there were no family plots to be buried in, the gravedigger would put the three side by side if it was the next place to dig graves," Carsten tried to console Emma with logic.

"Yes, I suppose. But to be buried beside the man who killed you?" Carsten felt Emma's shoulders shudder down to their clenched hands.

Carsten waited patiently as Emma, deep in thought, stared at the stones.

"Mama was in such deep shock that she didn't attend the burial. There wasn't a funeral for any of them anyway. It was a murder-homicide the town wanted to bury, literally," Emma said as she leaned over to touch her father's stone.

"Where were your grandparents?" Carsten asked, thinking of his large family, who would gather in support when someone died.

"All died in western Louisiana before Mama and Robert moved to Texas. My mother's brother, Sid Narker, had already moved to Austin, and Mama wanted to move close to him. Mama was happy when Papa was offered a teaching job in nearby San Antonio."

But then Sid had hired onto the Hamner cattle trail drive, headed for Kansas, leaving Sid's sister, Tina, to face her trauma by herself. Tina's travel to Kansas to meet her brother was how Tina had met Leif Hamner, her new husband, and Emma's stepfather.

Emma stood up and pointed to the new stone to the right of her father's.

"Rachel, wife of Simon Jarvis, 1875-1893. Oh, how sad, and only eighteen years old," Emma said as she leaned down to touch the woman's name."

"Do you know if George and Maria Jarvis had other children, besides their last infant that caused Mr. Jarvis' going crazy? Maybe an older son's wife was buried here because there was a plot available, closest to this Jarvis' couple," Carsten wondered out loud.

There were a couple of available spaces next to the Martin grave, typically left for a wife and possible child to be buried in the future. If the cemetery board knew that Tina left the area, maybe the gravesites were considered abandoned, allowing Simon Jarvis to claim the plots near his parents.

"I have no clue, other than the baby George Jarvis thought my father had sired. It makes sense that the plots were used because they were close to the Jarvis couple."

"Are you satisfied seeing your father's grave, or do you want to know more about it? Would you like to visit with Simon Jarvis?"

They were standing within a block of more information. Carsten was curious to meet Simon Jarvis. The man could give Emma more information about their fathers' connection if he agreed to meet with Emma.

Emma studied the four headstones before turning to Carsten. “I'd like to meet Simon Jarvis if he's willing to meet with me. Will you stay with me, though? I don't want to meet him alone.”

“Of course. I promised to be by your side the whole way,” Carsten replied as he squeezed Emma's hand.

Carsten was thinking about having Emma by his side longer than this trip, but time would tell.

Chapter 4

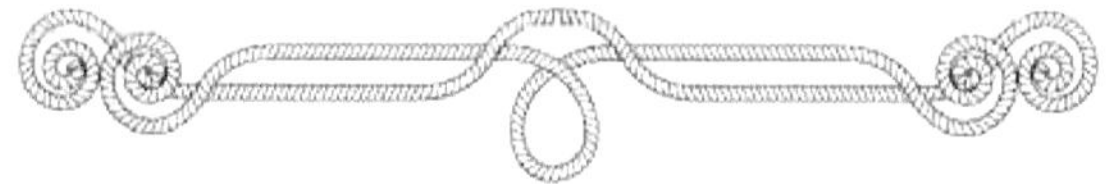

"May I help you?"

Emma stared, mouth gaping open at Simon Jarvis. They'd walked into the newspaper office asking if the man was available to visit with, and in from a hallway office walked the spitting image of her older brother.

"Uh, you're Simon Jarvis?" Carsten sputtered, just as surprised as she was. At least Carsten had found his voice. Emma couldn't utter a word to save her soul.

"Yes, sir. And you are Mr. and Mrs..." Mr. Jarvis asked, his hand still in the air because Carsten was still too much in shock to shake it.

"Brenner," Carsten finally said as he took the man's hand for his greeting.

"Well, Mr. and Mrs. Brenner, how can I help you?"

Neither she nor Carsten was in their right mind to correct Jarvis on their marital status.

The young man had dark blond hair, blue eyes, and was the mirror image of Emma's older brother, Robby.

Emma felt herself sliding down to the floor, but Carsten caught her.

"Ma'am, you're looking rather pale. May I offer you a chair in my office?" Jarvis hurriedly pointed to the open door down a short hall, and Emma felt Carsten guiding her in that direction.

"Miss Ferrell, could you please fetch a glass of water for this lady?" Emma heard Jarvis ask someone behind her as Carsten whispered, "Breathe, Emma. Don't pass out on me."

"I'm all right, Carsten," Emma protested as Carsten pushed her into the wooden chair in front of the office desk. Once seated, she grabbed Carsten's hand, as he began to push her head down between her knees.

"Carsten. Stop it," Emma whispered as Jarvis hurried into the room with a glass of water for her.

"Here you go. I'm so sorry if you're feeling under the weather?" Jarvis asked, looking at Emma and then at Carsten.

"And I'm sorry to scare you, Mr. Jarvis. But I just had a shocking—" Emma stopped and looked at Carsten, who now sat in the chair beside her, steadying her hand which was holding the glass of water.

Emma just had a fright? Shocking experience? What do you call meeting another brother?

"Take a few sips of water, Emma," Carsten encouraged her as he still held on to the glass as she lifted it to her lips.

Emma closed her eyes, drinking half the water before lowering the glass. She opened her eyes and faced the man now sitting at the desk, watching her with concerned eyes.

How could she go back and tell her mother that her first husband, Robert Martin, had indeed fathered a child with a Mrs. Maria Jarvis?

Tears welled in Emma's eyes, blurring her vision of the man staring at her.

"Emma, take deep breaths. You're hyperventilating now," Carsten said as he pried the water glass from her hand and set it on the edge of the desk.

"Emma, look at me," Carsten commanded as he pulled her hands toward him with one hand and used his other to touch her chin, so she'd turn her eyes toward him.

"How do I tell Mama? This news will crush her," Emma whimpered as tears flowed down her cheeks.

"Your mother is a strong woman who has gone through much worse. And this happened twenty years ago.

"Think about this instead, Emma. You have another brother," Carsten reminded her.

"*Excuse me?* What did you just say? Who *are* you?" Jarvis rose from his seat but sat back down when Carsten held out his hand to stop him from coming around his desk to confront them.

"Mind if I tell him what's going on, Emma?" Carsten quietly asked her as he stroked her cheek. All Emma could do was nod as she continued to cry.

"We just came from the cemetery down the street after visiting her father's grave. His name was Robert Martin, buried in between the Jarvis graves," Carsten flatly stated as Emma watched Jarvis' face.

"You are an identical twin in looks to Emma's oldest brother, Robert Martin Junior."

Jarvis fell back against his chair, his face struck with the news. Silence hung heavy in the air except for Emma trying to control her tears.

"Pull your family portrait out of your reticule, Emma," Carsten asked her, but she handed him the reticule for him to do it himself.

All she could think was, *how* could her father do this to her mother?

Carsten fumbled with her reticule strings to open it, but he finally pulled out the small portrait she had brought along to show the Ferguson family when they visited their ranch.

"Here's proof," Carsten said as he leaned over to hand the photograph to Jarvis. He reached for Emma's hand again before he continued. "Robby is first in line standing on the left, next to his and Emma's brother, Oliver. Emma is seated below them, beside her mother and her mother's second husband, Leif Hamner. Their two sons, Finn and Saul, stand behind Leif."

Jarvis stared at the photo while absently rubbing his chin. He looked up to study Emma's face, and she finally met his stare as she felt herself calm down. *Remember this happened twenty years ago.*

I have a fifth brother!

"Then, the mystery is solved. George Jarvis did kill my mother, and then my real father," Jarvis said slowly as he carefully laid the photograph on his desk.

Emma pulled her reticule off of Carsten's thigh and reached in it to pull out her handkerchief. She blew her nose as quietly as possible as she willed her composure, and her voice, to return.

"I'm sorry for my outburst, Mr. Jarvis. It was a shock as you do look exactly like my older brother," Emma explained.

"I see that," Jarvis said as he looked at the photograph and then met her eyes again. He did not look happy about the revelation.

"How old were you when this happened?" Emma inquired attempting to get the much-needed conversation going.

"Three days old, *sister* Emma," Jarvis drawled out slowly as he narrowed his eyes at her. "I assume I can call you by your given name now that we realize we're siblings."

"Well, *little brother*, Simon, I was a toddling two-year-old," Emma snapped back, not liking his tone.

"Where have you and your family been for the last twenty years? I was raised in an orphanage, with the stigma that my father was a murderous lunatic," Simon asked in a clipped voice. Emma could see his temper rising in his heated eyes. "Was my Martin family living in San Antonio this whole time?"

Emma stared at her brother, knowing they had so many questions that hours of conversation were needed to answer them.

"No, we've been in central Kansas. After my—our—father was killed, we left to travel to Kansas to meet my mother's brother, Sidney Narker. The train wrecked near Austin, and Robby and I were placed in an orphanage with the other children who had lost their parents in the horrible wreck.

"My pregnant and unconscious mother was taken to a saloon. There were so many injured people they were being placed wherever there was a bed available. She gave birth to our brother Oliver a few days later."

"How did you get back together?" Simon asked, now calmer as the news of their connection sunk in.

"A saloon worker took my newborn brother to the orphanage but was turned away because there were so many children taken there after the train wreck. Then the worker put the infant in the back of a covered wagon stopped at the store.

"A Mr. Leif Hamner found the infant in his wagon and tried to leave it at the same orphanage. After finally finding my mother in the saloon and picking up Robby and me at the orphanage, Leif took us on the cattle drive to Kansas. My mother married Leif, and we've lived on his ranch since then," Emma finished the abbreviated story of their arrival at their new home.

"You mentioned an uncle. Are there cousins or grandparents still living?"

"My uncle died before we reached Kansas, and we have no living grandparents, but I grew up as part of the Hamner family.

"Leif has two sisters and a brother, all with families of their own and ranching around us. Between the four siblings, there are twenty-four of us first cousins, all close. Oskar and Annalina Hamner, the siblings' parents, have always considered me their granddaughter."

"You mentioned growing up in an orphanage, Mr. Jarvis. I assume you had no older siblings then. Did you not have any family in the area?" Carsten asked, probably knowing Emma had more questions on her mind than she could ask.

"My ancestors were from Mexico, and my parents left the country after arguing with George's father. I never knew if any of my family was contacted after their deaths. If they were, they still didn't come to get me. I'm sure my mother giving birth to a blond, light-skinned baby was a disgrace to George Jarvis and his family."

Emma nodded, guessing how it had affected George and Maria's marriage, and her parents' too. Jarvis went into a rage and killed Simon's parents.

"How long have you been working for this newspaper?" Carsten asked, probably to get the tone back to civil between Simon and Emma.

"I was a newsboy, selling newspapers at a young age. The owner took me on as an apprentice when I was fourteen. It got me out of the orphanage. I still live in a room upstairs," Simon pointed a finger to indicate the second floor of the building.

"And we're probably keeping you from your work, Simon. Can we meet you for supper and visit more?" Emma asked, ready to rise and leave the room. She was in desperate need of fresh air.

"I need to pick up... Let's meet at the cafe, catty-corner of this building, at six o'clock. Does that work for you?"

Emma turned to Carsten, hoping he'd agree. It would be late before they could return to the depot where they left their luggage, but surely there was a hotel nearby where they could stay the night.

"Yes, that would work. Can you recommend a hotel near the depot for us to spend the night?" Carsten asked.

"The one across the street from the depot is clean and reasonable. How long are you staying in town?" Simon asked as he looked at the photograph again before handing it back to Emma.

Emma looked at Carsten, not sure what to say. "We planned to return home in ten days. After visiting my father's grave here, we plan to visit Austin. Besides seeing the orphanage where Robby and I lived for a short time, I want to visit the cemetery where my stepfather's first wife and infant son are buried.

"And Grandpa Hamner wants me to visit the Ferguson Ranch where the Hamner family lived and worked when they emigrated from Sweden. The Hamner family made trips once or twice a year with the Ferguson cattle drives after the Civil War until they bought their ranch in Kansas."

"I think staying in San Antonio to spend time with your brother is more important than visiting Austin, though," Carsten told Emma.

"I agree if you have time to visit with us this trip, Simon," Emma said, wanting to know her brother.

"This trip?" Simon asked, searching Emma's eyes for confirmation. "Will there be others?"

"Now that we've found you, expect to be visited by our family in the future, and I'd like to invite you to visit us in Kansas too," Emma promised as she stood on shaky legs. She needed to get out of the building before she collapsed with shock.

Carsten stood up and gently cupped her elbow, probably realizing she was quaking inside. "Nice to meet you, Simon," Carsten said as he held out his hand to shake Simon's. "We look forward to our evening meal and visit."

Carsten held on to Emma's elbow until they were outside on the sidewalk, and then he transferred her hand to the inside of his elbow.

"You are going to be all right, Emma? That was quite a shock to find you have a brother," Carsten told her as they walked down the street.

"I'm in shock and still thinking about how this affects Mama. I invited the man to visit us! How will she react to my invitation?"

"Your mother would do the same thing in the same circumstance. There will be no denying that Simon is related to your brother," Carsten said as he shook his head, still shocked by the uncanny resemblance to Robby.

"Oh, Carsten," Emma groaned as they started to pass the cemetery on their way back to the depot. "We didn't ask Simon about his wife. She's buried next to our father, and I didn't offer my condolences."

Carsten stopped and turned toward the rows of gravestones.

"No, we didn't, and he didn't say anything either, but we'll ask about the woman this evening. I think bringing up his deceased wife might have been too much for him to talk about with your revealment about your father."

"True. My head is reeling, and I imagine Simon's thoughts are worse than mine. To not know he had relatives this whole time?"

Emma leaned into Carsten's side; glad she had a hold of his arm. Carsten was becoming more than a childhood friend as he escorted her on this trip. What would it be like to be a couple when they traveled back home? Could Emma hope Carsten would want to court her? Or was he thinking about a different future than her or the Cross C Ranch?

Chapter 5

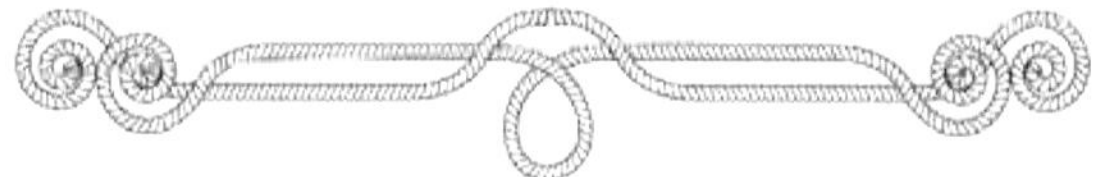

After going back to the depot to get their luggage, they acquired rooms for the night. Until they met with Simon this evening, they didn't know if they'd stay another day or head for Austin.

They found the schoolhouse's location where Emma's father had taught, but the building had been torn down and replaced with a two-story brick school sometime in the past two decades. Emma would have loved to have seen the house she was born in, but it was removed for the new school.

After revisiting her father's grave, they arrived at the cafe early to wait for Simon.

“I want to sit facing the door,” Emma said as she moved to the table and chair she wanted. Carsten could tell she was nervous, but she took a deep breath after he pulled out her chair, and she sat down.

“How do I look? Is my hat on straight?” Emma asked as she touched her hand to her hat again. She had changed from her light brown traveling dress to a cooler pastel green cotton calico when they were at the hotel.

"You look lovely, Emma. I like the color of your dress," Carsten said to calm her nerves. He enjoyed the blush that bloomed on her cheeks with his compliment.

"Thank you, Carsten. I'm still stunned that I have another brother. My heart is racing, and my stomach has butterflies—"

Carsten placed his hand over hers where she'd been tapping it on the table. "That's okay. I'm sure Simon feels the same way." He was pleased that she turned her hand over to grasp his fingers as he was glad she wanted his support.

"He's here," Emma said as the man walked through the door, carrying a baby. "Oh, my, he has a child?" Emma asked no one in particular as she stared at the infant in Simon's arms.

"That might explain his wife being buried in the cemetery," Carsten said under his breath as he rose to greet Simon.

"Good to see you again, Simon," Carsten said warmly as he waited for Simon to shift the baby into his other arm and shake his hand.

"Uh, thank you. This is my son, Paul," Simon said as he sat down in a chair and arranged the child on his lap.

"I have a nephew? Oh, he's precious. How old is he?" Emma gushed as she reached to brush her fingers over the baby's dark blond locks.

"Six months." Simon stared at his son without a feeling of warmth in his eyes.

"I'm guessing we owe our condolences to you for the passing of your wife?" Carsten asked and noticed Emma quickly glanced between him and Simon.

"Yes, my wife died six weeks after Paul was born," Simon said as he tightened his hold on his son. "She was very depressed after Paul's birth. I came home one evening from work to find she'd…passed."

"Oh, I'm so sorry, Simon. I wish I could have been here for you," Emma stated as she moved her hand from the baby's head to Simon's arm.

"Thank you. It would have been nice to have family here," Simon said with a slight edge to his voice. Carsten could tell Simon was still processing the news of his Martin connection to Emma and the sudden death of his wife too.

"Who takes care of Paul while you're at work?" Emma asked.

"He's with the wife of a fellow worker part of the day and sleeps in a backroom of the newspaper if I'm running the press at night."

The man's tired expression showed he didn't get enough sleep with limited help.

"May I hold Paul? I love babies," Emma said as she smiled at the baby and held out her arms.

"Sure," Simon said as he handed Paul to Emma.

The baby was silent as he stared up at Emma. Was he well cared for or needing more attention? Carsten thought Paul looked on the thin side.

"Does Paul's maternal family live in the area?" Emma asked as she played with Paul's fingers.

"No. Rachael was an orphan in the same orphanage where I lived. We married the day she turned eighteen and had to leave home. We weren't married long, but I still miss her."

"We saw her grave at the cemetery but forgot to mention it to you when we first met," Carsten confessed.

"She had to be buried somewhere, and there was a paid plot between the Martin and Jarvis graves," Simon shrugged.

"Hello, may I take your order?" a young waitress stood at their table, taking Carsten's attention away from Simon.

"What's the evening special?" Carsten asked, hoping the meal would improve this meeting.

"Roast, mashed potatoes, and carrots. Comes with coffee, buttermilk biscuits, and apple pie."

"The meal is my treat, Simon. Does the special sound good to everyone?" Carsten asked, and Emma and Simon nodded their acceptance.

"Three specials then. Simon, does Paul need a bottle of milk or a bowl of pureed food?"

"No, he ate before I picked him up."

"I'll share my potatoes with him. I assume he likes gravy and potatoes?" Emma asked as she cradled the baby.

"I assume so. Mrs. Elliot feeds him," Simon said as he sat back and the waitress arrived with a tray containing their coffee and biscuits.

"My sister and her husband adopted three children last fall. Your baby reminds me of my niece, Alice, as they are close to the same age," Carsten commented.

Alice was all smiles and plump arms and legs now, a contrast from Paul's thin limbs and quiet nature.

"Carsten has seven siblings and is a triplet. His sisters, Maggie, Molly, and Maisie, all married on the same day last fall. Two of the couples adopted children on that day off an orphan train," Emma said to get the conversation going again. "None of my siblings have married yet. Paul is my first nephew," Emma announced with a smile for the child.

Emma was a natural with the baby and would make a good mother someday.

"My siblings are a mix of children adopted by my adoptive parents, Marcus and Sarah Brenner. My widowed mother died after giving birth to us triplets, but it was because she'd fallen and hit her head on the stove before giving birth."

The tension in Simon's face eased with Carsten's mention of being orphaned and then adopted.

"Sounds like your life wasn't the best either?"

"No, my siblings and I have had a good life on the ranch. We were lucky the Brenner's took us in."

"Carsten and I grew up on neighboring ranches and have known each other since we were toddlers," Emma added to show their connection.

"That would have been nice, to be part of a close community," Simon sighed as he lifted his cup for another sip of coffee.

Carsten looked at Emma, who had a worried look on her face. This meeting wasn't going well. Was the man overtired or not interested in his long-lost family?

"Watch out. I'm sitting a hot plate in front of you, ma'am," the waitress warned Emma, who held the baby's hands down as she leaned back.

"Smells wonderful. Thank you," Emma thanked the waitress as she placed plates in front of Simon and Carsten next.

Paul's hands reached for the plate, but Emma was quick to pull him back. He made little grunting sounds as he tried to reach her mashed potatoes.

"I'd say he's hungry. May I feed him once the soft food cools down?" Emma asked Simon.

"Please, since he acts like he's starving. I worry if Mrs. Elliot is feeding him enough. He seems small compared to her toddler and baby. They are fat as butterballs."

"Are you sure Paul is getting adequate care? Is there someone else you could hire to take care of him?" Emma asked.

Carsten watched Emma mix a small amount of potatoes in the gravy on the edge of her plate. She scooped a bit of the mixture on the end of her spoon and blew on it before holding it in front of Paul. He lunged for the spoon in his awkward way, trying to suck the food into his mouth.

"No, I'm not sure about his care recently. Yesterday, Paul had a small bruise on his body, and Mrs. Elliot always brushes off my concerns, saying her toddler just played a little rough with him."

Emma pulled Paul into her chest with her left arm, showing protectiveness for her nephew.

"Surely you can find someone else to watch him for you?"

Simon buttered a biscuit before he answered Emma's question.

"Through no fault of my own, I don't have the best reputation in town. I was the son of George Jarvis, who murdered two people before taking his own life. I had the added stigma of growing up in Austin's worst orphanage, and I would guess the state. The home was not known for good food, clean beds, and loving caregivers.

"Finding a woman to take care of the baby of 'the son of a murderer' is hard."

Everyone grew quiet, eating their meal and ignoring Simon's comments. Emma continued to feed Paul between her bites of food. The baby had eaten most of Emma's mashed potatoes and gravy. Emma seemed satisfied with only eating her meat and vegetables.

Carsten asked questions about the city of Austin and Simon's work when their plates were cleared. But Simon's answers were brief as if the man could fall asleep at any moment instead of following the conversation.

They had just finished their pie when Simon stood and reached for Paul. "Thank you for the meal and visit, but I need to get back to work. We've had problems with the press today, and it will be a late-night catching up on printing tomorrow's issue."

"Simon, as your sister, I must say you look overworked. Is there another job that would suit you and Paul better?"

"The newspaper business is the only thing I know how to do. And I've explained why it's hard to find decent help for Paul. Good thing my salary includes the room upstairs, or I'd be more in a pickle than I am now," Simon sighed as he settled Paul against his shoulder.

"Then travel to Kansas with us. Move to be with family who could help take care of Paul," Emma blurted out.

Simon's eyes widened as Emma's words sunk in.

"Don't you think that's a good idea, Carsten?" Emma pleaded with him to help convince Simon of her sudden idea.

Carsten was cautious about agreeing because they didn't know the man yet. But Simon was Emma's relation. Shouldn't they offer help for that reason?

"It would be a good place to start a new life. You'd have the backing of the Hamner family and the community," Carsten suggested.

"What about your mother and stepfather, Emma? Would they welcome me into your family?"

Emma didn't hesitate a moment. "Yes, they would, Simon. Life dealt them hard blows, just like you, when they were in their twenties. They would support you if you moved to Clear Creek."

"I'd need a job and a place to stay. What are the possibilities of those needs?" Simon asked, looking more awake than he did while they ate their meal. Was he interested in starting over?

Carsten knew that Emma's house was full with all the adult children still living at home, but he knew he could offer shelter for them at the Cross C Ranch.

"Our family ranch home is huge and empty since four of my siblings have married and moved out," Carsten offered.

"His mother, Sarah, would be a wonderful caregiver for Paul while you lived there," Emma offered, knowing it would be correct. Carsten's mother would love to have a baby in the house again.

"I'd make a terrible ranch hand, though. I grew up in the city," Simon protested.

Dare Carsten suggest the perfect opportunity for him, though? Grandpa Isaac was funding the start of a newspaper in Clear Creek, but everyone expected Moses to start the newspaper once he came back from his trip to western Kansas.

"Oh! Simon could start the Clear Creek Courier!" Emma exclaimed, blurting out the information that Carsten wasn't sure they could offer to Simon. But there was a spark of interest in Simon's eyes at the possibility. Carsten didn't want to dim Simon's chance of a new life, but what if the position wasn't open?

Chapter 6

Oops. By Carsten's stare, she'd spoken out of line about the new newspaper Carsten's grandfather was starting in town. In her excitement, she forgot that Isaac was planning to start the business for Carsten's brother, Moses. Words were Moses' passion, and everyone assumed he'd want to run a newspaper instead of ranching for his living.

"Who named it the Clear Creek Courier?" Carsten asked as he avoided looking at Simon's interested look.

"Kaitlyn Reagan thought that would be a fitting name for a newspaper. Kaitlyn is the pastor's wife, Simon. Courier sounded like it would be the deliverer of fast and current news," Emma answered. "Hadn't you heard that gossip?"

"No, I hadn't. I'm guessing the Peashooter's Society hadn't finalized the details and announced it yet," Carsten retorted back.

"Your town is starting a newspaper?" Simon asked with more enthusiasm than he'd shown all evening.

"Yes, it's in the works. The building is almost done, but the equipment hasn't been ordered yet," Carsten cautiously told Simon. "Keep in mind this will be a very small newspaper, probably a weekly instead of a daily issue," Carsten added.

"Simon would know how to set up and run the press," Emma pressed on, hoping to entice her brother to think about it. Her brother and nephew needed to be with family. Surely Isaac would hire Simon, who knew the newspaper business, to help Moses set it up at least.

"Could you take time off work to travel home with us to visit family and check out the opportunity?" Emma suggested next, both to appease Carsten and to give another suggestion to Simon.

"I've never traveled out of state, let alone taken time off work," Simon shook his head.

Surely Simon took time off for his wife's death, but Emma didn't ask. She didn't want to remind Simon of the hard times he'd had in the past months.

"It would be a good move for your son, Simon," Emma added.

"When are you going back home? I couldn't leave tomorrow," Simon said as he gently rubbed Paul's back.

Emma looked to Carsten, but he shrugged his shoulders. "That's up to you, Emma."

"We could take the train to Austin tomorrow and spend a few days seeing that area to give you time to decide," Emma decided since Carsten gave her a choice.

"That might work. I'll ask my boss. And if I can't travel home with you this week, could I come for a visit in the near future? You said the newspaper equipment hadn't been delivered yet, so I'm assuming the paper wouldn't be up and running for at least a month or two," Simon calculated.

"I think you'd have more of an idea on the timeframe than we would, but a visit would be worth your time to at least meet your family," Emma pressed for Simon to think that way.

"If you'd like a suggestion of where to stay in Austin, my boss and I stayed at the Glover Hotel across from the depot when we were in town for business last year," Simon mentioned.

"Thanks for the recommendation. Could you send us a telegram in care of the hotel if you decide to travel with us now, or if you're coming at a later date? Then we'd know to wait for you in Austin or travel on home," Carsten asked.

Emma was glad Carsten was on board with Simon and his baby traveling with them. That would be her first choice, but a later visit would be welcomed too.

"I promise to send a telegram tomorrow evening with my answer," Simon said, smiling for the first time since they met him.

Emma stepped up to Simon and wrapped her arms around his waist, wanting to hug her brother.

"I'm so glad to have found you and Paul, Simon. Please consider visiting Kansas. Don't miss the opportunity to meet your brothers," Emma pleaded as she finally felt Simon's arm wrap around her.

"All right, you've convinced me. I'll try to get up there soon," Simon finally whispered above her head. All Emma could do is plant the idea in her brother's head.

"And you, little man, you need to eat more potatoes and gravy," Emma told Paul as she touched his nose.

"Sister Emma, I'll try to find another sitter if we don't travel with you this week."

"Good. Now we need to let you go to work. Thank you for meeting with us this evening. I'm so happy to find you," Emma said as she felt tears forming in her eyes. She stepped back to let Simon be on his way.

"I'll watch for your telegram, Simon. And I promise you and Paul are welcome to stay at the ranch house. My parents would be upset if I didn't extend their hospitality to you. That's just the way they are," Carsten said as he shook Simon's hand.

"Thanks to both of you. I'll see what my boss says and get back to you," Simon said as he stepped backward to reach the door and then walked out.

Emma turned after Simon left and hugged Carsten next. "I can't thank you enough for escorting me to San Antonio. If you hadn't, I never would have met my brother."

She stood on tiptoe to kiss Carsten's cheek, enjoying the smell of his bay rum toilet water on his face as she kissed him. Carsten wrapped his arms around her tightly and kissed her cheek too.

"You're more than welcome, Emma. I'm enjoying our adventure together," Carsten whispered in her ear, giving Emma shivers down her spine. She liked his attention. Did she dare tell him that?

"I like your hugs and kisses too," Emma whispered back, trying to ignore they still stood in the cafe with others around them.

Carsten pulled his head back to look at her but kept his arms around her shoulders.

"You do, huh? Think you'd like more of them both in the future?"

"Yes, I would, especially if you have a mind to court me," Emma boldly whispered.

"Let me pay the check, and we'll take a walk and talk about it," Carsten said as he stepped back and pulled money from his vest pocket. He laid the money on the table and held out his hand for her to take. Carsten pulled her toward the entrance, only letting go of her hand to pluck his hat off the coatrack, put it on his head, and open the door for them to leave.

They walked half a block before Carsten spoke.

"I've always liked you, Emma, but I didn't say anything since Beckett asked you out. Are you saying you'd prefer me to him?"

"Yes, I am," Emma laughed. "Beckett's enthusiastic personality wears me out just trying to keep up with his talking, where you always make me feel... I guess relaxed and secure," Emma wanted to say loved, but she didn't know if Carsten was giving her that kind of message or if she just wished for it.

"We've grown up together. Are you feeling a type of brotherly love toward me, or...something else?" Carsten asked as he squeezed her hand.

"Something else since I was thirteen," Emma answered as she shyly glanced in his direction.

"Thirteen, huh? I guess I was behind since I started liking you differently at age fifteen," Carsten said as he took her hand and wrapped it around his elbow.

Emma's heartbeat soared at their confessions. This was what she hoped would happen if they had time to be together without the group traveling with them.

"Are you interested in being a rancher's wife? I don't plan to do anything else with my life. Grandpa is giving all his grandchildren a place to live on the ranch or money to live elsewhere."

"Yes, I want to stay in the ranching community, but now it makes me sad to think how well our lives turned out versus Simon's. He's had no one, *ever*, to care for him." Emma leaned into Carsten's side as they slowly walked down the street. Even if something would happen to her husband at an early age, she'd still have a family to help her.

"You're a good woman, Emma. I'm proud of you for offering your family's help to Simon. I'm sorry I was a little slow to offer it right away."

"We don't know the man, but there is no question he's my brother. I hope my family will give him a chance. He was an innocent baby and didn't deserve any discrimination."

"That's true. Let's hope Simon decides to travel with us. I doubt Simon realizes how hard it would be to travel alone with an infant," Carsten said as they strolled down the street. She liked holding on to Carsten's arm dreaming they were engaged to be married.

"Are you daydreaming, Emma?" Carsten asked as he patted her hand.

"What? I guess I wasn't listening. I was enjoying our evening walk." And thinking of something other than Simon and Paul at the moment.

"I said I don't think Simon knows how hard it would be to travel alone while caring for an infant."

"Women do it all the time. You think men can't do it?" Emma teased Carsten.

"I confess I'd have a hard time, but then Simon has been taking care of Paul by himself for a while, so maybe my thinking he'd need help on the trip is hasty."

"As tired as Simon looked this evening, I'd say he'd sleep most of the train trip to Kansas," Emma sighed. Her brother looked past the point of exhaustion.

"In the meantime, we can travel to Austin tomorrow morning to see the town."

"Since San Antonio has grown and it was hard to find the sites Mama talked about, I'm betting Austin will be the same way," Emma mused. At least she wouldn't expect the buildings to be exactly as her parents described them now.

"True. The cemetery may be the only thing that hasn't been altered in twenty years. Are you going to be disappointed if that happens?" Carsten asked as they waited for the streetcar to pull to a stop. They would board it for their ride back to the hotel.

"Not after seeing the growing city of San Antonio. We'll see the Hamner graves in the cemetery and then have time to hire a buggy to visit the Ferguson Ranch too."

They took a bench seat on the streetcar, and Carsten wrapped his arm around the back of the seat, pulling her close to kiss her cheek.

"Sounds like a good plan. And if we hear from Simon that he won't be joining us on our trip home, maybe we can explore another town on the way? We could stop in Fort Worth, Oklahoma City, or Wichita. We still have extra days before we meet our brothers and cousins."

"Let me guess. You want to see the Fort Worth Stockyards," Emma laughed.

"I am a cattleman, and I'm sure the stockyards are impressive. Actually, I've been looking forward to this trip to Texas since our grandpas suggested it. This area is where the Longhorn cattle drives started. Can you imagine following a massive herd of animals for months as they walk from Texas to Kansas?"

"I was on a trail drive with Mama and the Hamners when I was two years old, but I don't remember any part of it. Robby remembers flashes of scenes, being two years older."

"Like what?"

"Robby is deathly afraid of rattlesnakes because of that trip. Leif stopped the wagon when we children needed a potty break and didn't realize he'd stopped near a den of snakes. Robby had his pants down and almost got bit."

"Bet that scared the daylights out of your parents."

"Mama shudders whenever that story is mentioned. It scared the horses to the point they pushed back on the braked wagon, causing it to almost run over Leif and me. Leif shot the rattler closest to Robby but missed and shot the dog instead, who had lunged at the snake to protect Robby," Emma went on with the story.

"Was that Samson, the dog who followed you from the orphanage?"

"Yes. Samson was the huge brown dog we had for years. We thought he might have had some mastiff breed in him. We've had a lot of dogs on the ranch over the years, but I think he's still my favorite."

"This is the stop where we get off, Emma," Carsten said as he stood and helped her off the streetcar. "Let's stop at the depot and find out the schedule for tomorrow's train to Austin."

"Good idea. I'd like to leave on an early train if we can."

"It will be interesting to see Austin, but I don't expect the town to reveal as much information as San Antonio did," Carsten warned her as he switched places with her, so he was on the outside edge of the sidewalk.

Emma looped her hand around Carsten's elbow as they walked toward the depot. "I doubt anything can top finding a long-lost brother and nephew. I'm so glad we traveled to Texas."

"I wonder what the other couples are doing right now?" Carsten asked as he covered his hand over hers.

"I bet Asher and Alva are still in an exhibit hall, and Beckett and Greta have already toured horse farms around Louisville," Emma laughed, knowing the couples would have been bored walking through a cemetery with them.

"Thank goodness Greta is wild about horse racing. We've been on our own, and I have you all to myself," Carsten said as they stopped in front of the depot.

"And I've loved being with you," Carsten said before lowering his head and kissing her on the lips.

Emma's lips tingled after Carsten finally pulled away and opened the depot door for her. Greta may be wild about horse racing, but Emma was becoming fascinated with Carsten's kisses.

Chapter 7

Carsten stood to the side as Emma crouched down to touch the gray granite headstone which had, "Britta Hamner and infant son, Johan Karl" carved on its front. Dirt and lichen had crept into the crevasses of engraved words on the stone, giving them a sense of age.

What would it feel like to stand in this spot as your wife and son were buried? Carsten closed his eyes, trying to imagine the pain and emptiness Leif would have felt the day of the burial. Leif would have been in his twenties, only married a short time, but still, to have your wife and son die in the act of childbirth must have been gut-wrenching.

"Leif was so young when this happened, but I think it shaped the man he became. He was so worried when Mama was pregnant with Finn and Saul," Emma said as she traced the names with her index finger.

"Life events do change and alter one's life," Carsten said as he scanned the cloudy sky above them. Accidents took both of his parents when they were young too.

This time it was easy to find the correct cemetery when they arrived in Austin. Once Carsten mentioned they were looking for the cemetery where the 1873 train wreck victims were buried, the older depot manager gave them directions.

They checked into the hotel Simon had mentioned, ate lunch in their hotel's dining room, then made their way to the cemetery.

"If it weren't for Leif, I would have grown up in the orphanage," Emma mused as she rose and stepped back from the stone.

Carsten wrapped his arm around her middle and gave her a sideways hug. "You'd have been adopted by someone since I bet you were a darling toddler."

"With a broken leg and cuts all over my face?" Emma asked as she shook her head.

"You healed. That's what counts," Carsten said as he looked to the next row of graves containing the train wreck victims. Carsten counted twenty-nine graves, many of them not marked with a named stone. If Emma had been one of the dead, he never would have met her, and that caused his chest to ache.

"So many families were shattered by the train wreck. I've often wondered how many injured people were in homes or businesses while their spouse or child was buried here," Emma said as she leaned her head on Carsten's shoulder.

"I bet we can find out more information from the local newspaper. It would be in their archives."

"Think I'd find another brother there too?" Emma asked as she shook her head at the notion.

"I think it's safe to say you won't find family here, but I've learned to never say never on this trip."

"So true. Could you find a florist and bring flowers back to the grave tomorrow?" Emma looked up to Carsten to ask.

"I was thinking along that line too, but then we passed a greenhouse on the way here. They'd have perennials or a rose bush we can plant on Britta and Karl Johan's grave instead."

"And let us borrow a shovel too?"

"I think they would, and if not, we can borrow one from the cemetery's sexton." Carsten would buy a shovel if he had to plant whatever Emma wanted to decorate the grave with.

"The cemetery is lush with new green grass now, but summer heat changes the growing conditions. Even if it weren't the right time of year to plant them, a peony or clump of irises would survive for years," Emma suggested.

"True. Think of all the irises growing in the Clear Creek cemetery. Edna Clancy planted yellow irises on her son's grave when his death started the town cemetery in the late 1860s. That area of the cemetery is a wash of yellow blooms each year," Carsten said, thinking of the colorful cemetery each May. Now there were more colors of irises and peonies as people planted flowers around their loved one's graves.

"Maybe what we plant at Britta's grave would spread to the train victims' section."

"Maybe we buy extra plants and spread the future color ourselves," Carsten said, thinking ahead to decorating the section.

"You're so thoughtful, Carsten. One of the many qualities I admire about you," Emma said before rising on her toes to kiss him. Carsten pulled her against his chest, relishing the close connection they'd made on this trip, and deepening the kiss.

Emma groaned her satisfaction instead of pushing Carsten away. He'd plant a clump of irises on each grave if she'd kiss him for each one.

After indulging in having Emma in his embrace, Carsten reluctantly stepped back. They had more stops for their day besides the cemetery.

*

"Are you sure this is the right corner?" Carsten asked as he pulled the horse and buggy he rented for the afternoon to a stop.

Emma looked at the piece of paper and read out loud. "The saloon is two blocks west and two blocks north of the cemetery, on the northwest corner of the intersection."

"We passed the mercantile Leif talked about so this should be, or was, the saloon."

But instead of the building, there was a pile of freshly burned wood on that corner.

"Looks like it happened not too long ago. Surely it would have been cleaned up by now otherwise," Carsten surmised as he surveyed the damage. Beams of charred wood, probably from the second story, lay haphazardly on top of the first-floor rubble. A tumble of bricks on the building's alley side was what was left of the kitchen fireplace chimney. The air still had a slight stench of burned wood too.

"Let's go back to the mercantile and ask the clerk if it was the Bailey Saloon," Emma asked as Carsten signaled to the horse to move on. They circled the block looking for the name on another building but didn't see it.

"The business could have changed names, or maybe Leif didn't remember the correct location."

"But the mercantile location was right," Emma replied as she turned to look up and down the street again.

What was the chance the building Emma wanted to see burned down the same week they were in Texas to see it? Carsten blew out a breath as he reined the horse around the corner to return up the street again.

Carsten stopped in front of the mercantile, braked the buggy, and jumped down from his side of the vehicle to take care of the horse.

"Don't get your hopes up, Emma," Carsten warned her as he helped her off the buggy. "It's possible it's been another business for years."

"That could be, but I still want to know."

Carsten tucked Emma's hand around his elbow and escorted her into the mercantile.

An older man looked up from the counter when the doorbell announced their presence.

"May I help you?" the storekeeper asked as Carsten led Emma to the counter.

"Yes, sir. We're from out of town and wondering what was the business that burned on the corner. Was it by chance the Bailey Saloon?"

"Yes, it was. It burned the night before last. We were lucky the whole block didn't burn down. The fire department managed to put it out but wasn't able to save the people sleeping upstairs," the storekeeper shook his head.

"Oh, how terrible! How did the fire start?" Emma gasped in horror.

"Not sure. It was a hot fire, and it's hard to tell what happened.

"What a terrible situation for the people who died and their family members," Emma said as she shook her head.

The man coughed in his hand. "Well, being they were, ah, saloon girls, I don't think they had a family to worry about them."

"That's not always true. My mother was in the saloon, and she had family," Emma firmly stated as she stared at the man.

The man looked bug-eyed at her. "Your mother worked there?"

"No," Carsten said to clear the confusion. "Her mother was in the train wreck that happened here twenty years ago, and she was cared for at the Bailey Saloon until she was reunited with her family."

"Oh, yes, that was a terrible calamity. Four passenger cars rolled off a bridge into a creek. So many people died and were injured. Your mother was one of the people who survived?"

"Yes, although her back was injured. She gave birth to my little brother in the saloon a few days after the accident."

"Emma and her brother were taken to an orphanage near here since her mother was unconscious," Carsten added to the story.

"That would be the old orphanage, two blocks west of the south corner," the storekeeper told them.

"Is the home still there?" Emma leaned against the counter to ask the man.

"It is, but it's no longer in use since a new orphanage is just opening up. Miss Robertson decided to retire instead of moving to the new home."

"Had this Miss Robertson been at the home for a long time?" Carsten asked. "Maybe she took care of you and Robby, Emma."

"Very possible. Miss Robertson's been there for many years. If you want to visit her, she hasn't moved out yet. Look for a faded gray house on the south side of the street. It's two-story, with a small porch out front," the shopkeeper told them.

"Thank you for the information, sir," Carsten said as he guided Emma out the front door and then helped her back into the buggy.

"I assume the orphanage is our next stop, or are you ready to go back to the hotel?" Carsten asked as he stepped up into the buggy.

"I want to visit with Miss Robertson now if she's available. My mind has been brimming with questions about the orphanage for years."

Chapter 8

"It's not as large as I thought it would be," Emma said as they stood in front of the orphanage. It was nothing more than a two-story home in dire need of painting.

"But I bet the irises around the foundation were pretty last month," Carsten said, trying to make Emma feel better.

Yes, a thick bed of irises snaked around the whole house, but the spent stalks needed to be trimmed out. There were a few late blooms that showed they were varieties of yellow and purple.

Emma walked up to the door, took a deep breath, and used the door knocker to announce their arrival.

"Don't expect much, Emma. It was twenty years ago when you stayed here," Carsten warned her, but he laid his hand on her lower back to show his support. She couldn't have made this trip without Carsten.

"Yes, may I help you?" an older woman with a buxom figure and curly gray hair asked as she opened the door and saw them on the porch.

Emma froze. This woman would have taken care of her and Robby twenty years ago after the train wreck.

"Good afternoon, ma'am. We're looking for a Miss Robertson," Carsten came to her rescue since her tongue was tied.

"I'm Miss Verna Robertson," the woman stated and waited for one of them to proceed.

Carsten looked at Emma and then continued for her since the situation of her past left her mute.

"I'm Carsten Brenner, and this is Emma. She was one of the children who spent time here after the train wreck in 1873."

"Oh, my word! Please, come in! I'm delighted to see a former resident again," Miss Robertson's smile broke the lump in Emma's throat.

"Thank you, Miss Robertson. My brother and I were here for a short time until my mother claimed us."

"Oh, you didn't stay long? I'm so happy you were one of the fortunate ones. I had a few girls stay for years," the woman replied as she led them into a sitting room and motioned for them to sit down on the settee. "Would you like a cup of tea? I always have hot water on the stove."

The woman sounded happy to have company, and Emma realized the house was quiet. Were there no longer any children living here?

Leif remembered there were so many children in the house it was near overflowing.

"Oh, please don't go to the trouble. We were in the area and wanted to visit," Emma said awkwardly.

"I'd like a glass of water, though, if you don't mind," Carsten asked as he smiled at the woman.

"Just one moment then," Miss Robertson said as she left the room.

"Why did you ask for a drink, Carsten? The woman doesn't move well and—"

"Because you needed a moment to catch your breath. Ever since you saw the house, you've been close to hyperventilating."

"It's just overwhelming. My brain is racing with thoughts and questions," Emma whispered.

"I know. Take a deep breath and let it out. Relax."

"Here you go, Mr. Brenner. I must say I'm pleased you stopped by. I rarely have visitors anymore."

"Do you still have children in the home? It's quiet," Carsten asked before taking a sip of water.

"No, I don't. I used to be overwhelmed with taking care of children some days and wished for a bit of silence. I must say I'm enjoying the quiet house now that my last ward left recently."

"Is there no longer a need for an orphanage?" Emma asked, hoping that was the case.

"No, there is a new home on the other side of town, but I won't be moving there. I've been in the process of cleaning out this house, then planning to move in with my older sister."

"That's wonderful for you and your sister," Emma said politely as she wondered how to start her questions.

"Do you remember taking care of a two-year-old girl with a broken leg and her four-year-old brother after the train wreck? That was my brother Robby Martin and myself," Emma asked as she searched Miss Robertson's face for any sign of remembering.

The woman's eyebrows moved downward as she thought. "Do you know how long you were here?"

"I don't think more than a week or so. My mother was injured and taken to the Bailey Saloon, not realizing we'd survived. She gave birth to my little brother, Oliver, in the saloon.

"A saloon worker, Amy Fisher, well that's her married name now, brought Oliver here, but you didn't have room for him."

"Amy Sanders by chance? Huh. I haven't thought of her for years. She just disappeared one day," Miss Robertson looked off to the distance.

"Anyway, Amy put Oliver in the back of my stepfather's wagon, afraid to take the baby back to the saloon. His name is Leif Hamner, a very tall blond man."

"Yes! I remember the young man! He brought the baby, then left...bringing the mother and infant back here. *You* were the little girl he came back to get?" Miss Robertson said as she clapped her hands. "Where did you go after you were reunited?"

Emma relaxed, now happy to tell the rest of the story.

"Leif took us with him to catch up with his family's cattle trail ride to Kansas. Mama and Leif married and had two sons, Finn, and Saul. We live on a ranch surrounded by other members of the Hamner family. Our tragedy turned into a happy ending."

"Back to Amy, how do you know about her? I always felt sorry for the young woman."

"Mama sent Amy money for her helping, then Amy disguised herself as a young man and rode with a carload of bulls to Kansas. She married my uncle's ranch foreman, Eli Fisher, and they have several children."

"I'm so glad to hear about Amy. And I can't tell you how happy I am that you've had a good life. I always worried when children came into my care. I know some babies were adopted into good homes, and others…." Miss Robertson shook her head.

"Except for the train wreck victims, I understood from Mrs. Fisher that the majority of babies came from the saloons?" Emma asked, curious about the orphanage's past.

"Yes, it's true of that time period. Some of the saloon owners insisted the working women gave up their babies so they could keep working.

"Mr. Bailey was an especially stern saloon owner, but if I ever needed anything for the children, he'd furnish it. Clothes, food, Christmas toys."

But apparently not paint and upkeep on the orphanage home, though.

"We drove past the Bailey Saloon before we stopped here. What happened to the place?" Carsten asked.

Tears welled in Miss Robertson's eyes. "I never condoned the saloons, but it was such a tragic event. Mr. Bailey and four women were asleep upstairs when the fire broke out in the early morning day before last. I honestly believe it was arson, although the police aren't taking the matter seriously. The mayor has been on a tear to clean out that part of town, and it was 'convenient' that a fire started. I think he was hoping the whole block would burn."

"I'm sorry for the loss of life. We did see a few fresh graves when we visited the cemetery today. My step-father's first wife and son are buried there, and we stopped to pay our respects."

"That was very commendable of you to visit the cemetery," Miss Robertson said, and then cocked her head to the side. "You know, I've been cleaning out the house because it's going to be razed this summer. A new brick schoolhouse will be built on this lot. There are some boxes up in the attic you might be interested in. I haven't carried them downstairs yet."

Emma's heart sank at the idea the home was going to be torn down, but Miss Robertson's twinkling eyes didn't hold any sorrow.

"If the house is going to be torn down, may I dig up some iris rhizomes and move them to the cemetery?" Carsten asked. "Emma and I were just talking about how Mrs. Hamner's grave, and the train wreck victims' graves, should have some perennials planted around them. I was going to check with the greenhouse we saw to buy some plants, but if I may, I'd like to transfer irises to the cemetery tomorrow."

"That's a splendid idea. There are several peony bushes on the backside of the house you might try moving too. I know they should be transplanted in the fall, but they'll be in the way of the demolition and rebuilding. Might as well try to save them."

Emma waited patiently, wanting to get back to the topic of the boxes in the attic.

"You were saying something about boxes I could look at? What do they contain?"

"Things salvaged from the train wreck were brought here because the children needed clothing, their own, or what we could find to fit. But I know there were personal items we kept because they might have belonged to the children's families."

"We were on that train because we were moving from San Antonio to Kansas. *Everything* we owned was on the wrecked train," Emma exclaimed.

"I'm sure your clothes would have been used for many youngsters until they were threadbare. But I also saved any personal items that I could match with the children," Miss Robertson said with a knowing smile.

"Could you still have my family photographs? Mama has lamented over the years that she lost them in the train wreck."

"Mr. Brenner, would you be so kind as to bring down the boxes from the attic? You're just the man I've needed for the project. If you have time to do it today?"

"Yes, we do. About how many boxes are you talking about, and where shall I stack them?" Carsten offered with a smile. Emma was proud of his willingness always to help out anyone with any project.

"Is now the right time to confess I haven't been in the attic for years and don't remember how much is up there?" Miss Robertson laughed. "I'll show you the staircase to the attic and let you see for yourself. You can stack the boxes in the dining room along the wall. That way, we can spread things out on the table to go through them."

What luck to visit Austin this spring. If they had come later, the orphanage, Miss Robertson, and her knowledge, would have been gone.

The three of them stood just as the door knocker quietly echoed through the living room.

"Goodness. I haven't had a visitor in a week, and today I have two. Excuse me a moment."

Emma felt Carsten's hand stroke her back and relaxed into it.

"We can stay here as many days as you want, Emma. We can send a telegram to let Asher and Beckett know we're extending our visit."

"What about Simon, though? He and Paul might be here tomorrow evening."

"We can all stay here in Austin for a few days if need be. Simon looks like he could use some sleep before we travel on to Kansas anyway. Or, he can help me clean out the attic. I'm a little worried that boxes and crates might be piled to the rafters."

"Mrs. Ellis! What in the world?"

Emma and Carsten turned to walk to the front door at Miss Robertson's exasperated question.

In the doorway stood a woman, holding out a toddler, wrapped in a burlap bag. The woman looked like she was holding a smelly bag of garbage in front of her and didn't want it touching her.

"I found her behind our trashcans in the alley. I bet she was one of the saloon girls' brats," the woman snipped.

"Mrs. Ellis, she's an injured child! Look at the burns on her face and arms! Why didn't you take her to the doctor?"

"You were closer and have always taken care of the saloon's outcasts. Take the baby, or I'll leave her on the porch," Mrs. Ellis warned Miss Robertson.

The child's eyes opened, and as she looked around the room, her eyes widened upon seeing Emma.

"Mama?" The injured child hoarsely cried as she tried to reach for Emma with her dirty hand.

Chapter 9

Emma reacted immediately, gently taking the child and holding her against her chest, not mindful of the dirty sack or child.

"Are you the mother? Why was she in the alley?" Mrs. Ellis peppered Emma with berating questions.

"No, she isn't the child's mother, but a more concerned woman for the injured toddler than you are," Carsten raised his voice to put the woman in her place. "We just arrived from out of state to visit Miss Robertson."

"Oh. Well, excuse me, young lady. You look like the woman they called Raven when they came into our dry goods store, but then, she died in the fire," Mrs. Ellis said as she stepped back onto the porch.

"I knew the saloon women by sight, but I didn't realize one of them had kept a baby. Tell me what you know about the child, Mrs. Ellis. You owe me that for bringing her here," Miss Robertson wearily asked.

How many times over the years had the orphanage's caregiver been in this situation?

"I didn't know they had a baby in the saloon either. I didn't look the child over very well, but I think her injuries are only on her body's upper part. Being burned, she *had* to come from the saloon. My guess is that she was dropped from the second story of the saloon in a blanket or something, and she crawled away from the fire."

Emma swayed her body to calm the sobbing child who had nestled her head in the crook of Emma's neck.

"Do you think Raven was the mother?"

"I do, and maybe Mr. Bailey was the father, and that's why the baby was still at the saloon. The man was in his sixties, but he was partial to the young black-haired woman. I'd see him and Raven walking together some early mornings before the saloon opened for the day."

"And they are both gone now," Miss Robertson said with a nod. "I owe it to Mr. Bailey to find a home for his child. Thank you, Mrs. Ellis, for bringing her here."

"Wait," Emma asked as the woman turned to leave. "Do you happen to know the child's name?"

"No, I don't," Mrs. Ellis said as she quickly walked down the porch steps.

"What can we do to help you take care of the child?" Emma quickly offered.

"Let me gather up some things, and I'll meet you in the bathroom, which is the small room off the kitchen," Miss Robertson said after a moment. "I no longer have any children's clothing here, but I'll find something to dress her in. Towels are in the small closet across from the bathroom door."

Miss Robertson was in her caretaker mode as she started up the steps of the house.

Carsten walked down the hall toward the back of the house until he found the bathroom and the closet across from it.

"In here," Carsten motioned to Emma as she continued swaying down the hall. The poor child was wailing as loud as her smoke-damaged lungs could manage.

The light from the window in the room showed a toilet, sink, tub, and a small table large enough to lay a baby on and change its diaper. Carsten spread a towel on the table as Emma one-handedly tried to pull the gunny sack off the child's back.

"Here, let me help you, Emma. She's scared and in pain."

They worked together to get the rough sack, dirty dress, and filthy diaper off the child.

"Oh, no. Look at her sore little bottom!" Emma cried as she laid the child on her front against the table. Tears were starting to form in Emma's eyes for the poor child's condition.

Carsten was handy at changing Maggie's two young children's diapers, but this brown-crusted red-flaming skin was almost more than he could handle.

"I'll start the water in the tub," Carsten said as he turned away to get his rolling gut to calm down.

"Keep it lukewarm, and don't add more than an inch or two of water. We'll need to drain the dirty water and draw fresh a time or two as we clean her."

The child continued to cry and try to curl up in a ball as Emma held her down on the table, waiting for the water to flow into the tub.

"I'll hold her standing in the water while you wash her body," Carsten offered as he picked up the little girl and then knelt beside the tub. "I've got two wash cloths already hanging on the side of the tub. I saw a bar of soap on the edge of the sink."

"Ready?" Emma asked as Carsten changed places with her to pick up the child.

"Ready," Carsten replied as he picked up the little girl. Her torso and legs were only dirty, except for her inflamed little bottom. The delicate skin on her face's right side, including her ear, was reddened, and blistered. The dark locks on the right side of her head were scorched short. Her hands and right arm were scratched and bleeding, but none of them looked infected, well, except for one spot on the palm of her right hand once he looked at it closer.

"Hey, little girl. I got you. Miss Emma is going to make you feel better," Carsten spoke softly, trying to calm her down. Once the washcloth touched her backside, though, she kicked her feet in the water to get away, soaking Carsten's arms and shirt as he held on to the fighting child.

"Hey, Sweetie. Dolly. Baby," Carsten continued to say nicknames she might recognize, but that wasn't working as the panicked child continued to fight.

"Try singing, Carsten. Anything from a lullaby to a tune you'd hear in a saloon. Maybe Camptown Races?"

"I'm not going to sing that song to her, even though she might know it. How about, Twinkle, twinkle, little star, how I wonder what you are!" Carsten starting singing, and the girl turned to watch his mouth.

"Up above the world so high, like a diamond in the sky.

"When the blazing sun is gone, when he nothing shines upon, then you show your little light, twinkle, twinkle, all the night."

The toddler quit screaming, but it might have been because Emma was softly rubbing her tummy now instead of her being mesmerized by Carsten's singing.

Carsten sang the verses he knew over and over while they worked together to clean the child up.

"I didn't ask if you two had any children," Miss Robertson said from the hallway. "You make a good team."

"Just lots of nephews and nieces, all adopted last fall, actually," Carsten replied, for some reason not wanting to deny they were married.

Emma started to speak up about their marital status but just smiled instead once she saw Carsten's raised eyebrows. Maybe Miss Robertson didn't think it was proper for them to bathe a child together if they weren't married.

Carsten reached with one hand to pull the plug to drain the third round of water from the tub while Emma gently patted the child dry while she still stood in the tub.

"I'll pick her up, and you can dry her legs and feet," Carsten said as he lifted the girl and placed her on his chest, careful not to anchor her by her sore bottom.

The child went limp against him in exhaustion, the fight going out of her now that she was clean and held.

"Mr. Brenner, please bring her into the kitchen and lay her on the table. I have a salve for her wounds."

Carsten carried the girl into the kitchen, where Miss Robertson had already laid out a towel, diaper, and he guessed one of Miss Robertson's blouses.

"Do I need to fetch a doctor?" Carsten asked, ready to do whatever the little girl needed. He thought she'd recover without seeing one, but he'd be glad to do whatever Miss Robertson asked of him.

"I think she'll heal fine, but I'll have to watch for infection. She's got to be dehydrated and hungry too," she said, as she took the girl from his arms.

The toddler shrieked at being moved until Carsten held out his hand to her, and she curled her left hand around one of his fingers. Carsten started humming the twinkle song again as he stayed in contact with her, and she calmed down more.

"I'm guessing she's just under two years of age," Miss Robertson said as she finished clothing the child and wrapping her in a soft blanket.

"You seem to be her champion, Mr. Brenner, so please take her and sit down while I finish her oatmeal."

"I made myself at home in your kitchen and have a glass of water and a bowl of food ready for her," Emma said as she sat down at the kitchen table with the glass and bowl.

"Thank you to both of you. While you're feeding her, I'm going downtown to find out who she is. There has to be someone else who knew of her existence at the saloon."

The older woman pushed her hat on her head, stuck a pin through it and her hair to keep it on, and purposefully strolled out the front door.

"I'd say Miss Robertson has been a champion and savior for many orphans in this part of town," Emma said as she held the glass up for the girl to drink out of. The girl gulped the water so fast she started to choke.

"Slow down, little girl. Take your time," Carsten said as Emma moved the glass out of the girl's reach.

"Wa, wa," the toddler barely whispered and tapped the side of her face.

"Yes, here's more water. I'll give you milk with your oatmeal next."

Carsten was settled in a rocker in the living room with the toddler fast asleep on his chest when Miss Robertson came home. Emma, who had been cleaning up the kitchen, walked in from the kitchen when she heard the woman's arrival.

"I visited with the former saloon cook. The child's name is Anna, born in October of 1891, so she's not quite two years old. Her mother was Dorothea, although she went by Raven. The cook said she didn't know the woman's last name or where she came from.

"No one knew for sure who her father was, but everyone knew Mr. Bailey had a soft spot for the girl, so I'm guessing the adults were, let's say together, and leave it at that," Miss Robertson said as she sat down on the settee beside Emma.

"What happens to Anna now that you're ready to retire? Does she have to go to the new orphanage?" Emma asked with worry in her eyes.

Carsten hugged Anna closer to his chest, wanting to give her a sense of peace and safety, even if she was sleeping.

Miss Robertson studied Anna in his arms before turning to stare at Emma.

"Mr. Brenner. When we talked about your family in Kansas, didn't you say your sisters adopted children last year?"

"Yes, orphans from New York, right off the train. All five are wonderful children, although Molly's twin boys are a handful at age six. Maggie has two little girls, one a little younger and one a little older than Anna, and a four-year-old boy."

Miss Robertson sat back in the settee, tapping her chin in thought.

"I can't take a child because my plans of retiring are in place. Instead of taking Anna to the new orphanage, I suggest you and your husband adopt her, Emma. I think you're the type of person who would like to pay forward for the care you and your brother were given here. Am I correct?"

Emma's eyes widened and turned to find Carsten's eyes at Miss Robertson's suggestion.

Wait. Did Miss Robertson say *you and your husband*? And suggest *they,* as in Emma and himself, raise Anna as their own?

Carsten guessed letting Miss Robertson think they were married wasn't a good idea after all.

Chapter 10

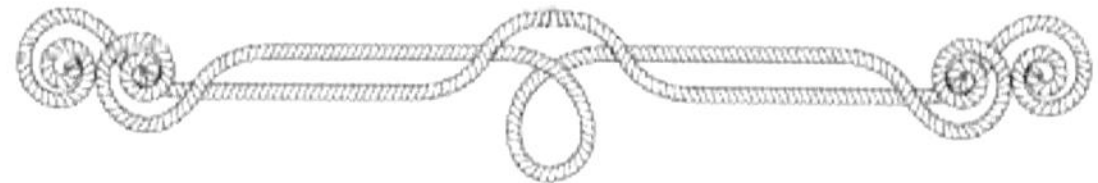

"I think the photographs I need to show you are in that trunk," Miss Robertson pointed to one of the many crates and trunks Carsten had carried down from the attic and stacked in the dining room. Most of the trunks were filled with blankets and coats only used during the winter. Carsten also carried down a dozen folded cots, probably used when the orphanage had an overflow of children. Some of them were old enough that Emma and Robby might have slept on them too.

Emma could tell by Carsten's footsteps on the stairs up to the attic that echoed through the house that he was tired from the multiple steps he'd taken today. But when Miss Robertson suggested Carsten stop, he said he was determined to bring it all downstairs before daylight ran out.

Anna slept restlessly on Carsten's chest for the first hour after they cleaned her up. After that, she slept in Emma's arms a while before settling on Miss

Robertson's ample bosom. Anna wanted to be held instead of lying down on a bed, so they had accommodated her for now. The poor child was hurt inside and out by her battered body and sad heart.

Anna had asked a few times for her momma and her auntie, whoever that was, but all they could do was shush her and sway her back to sleep.

"This box?" Emma asked after she'd opened the trunk Miss Robertson had pointed to and pulled out a small wooden box.

"Yes, bring it over to the table, and we'll sort through it. There weren't any pictures in the last trunk I thought they were in, so I hope we have luck with this one."

"What are you going to do with all this stuff?" Emma asked.

"Well, at this point, I just as well burn what I can't pass on to the new orphanage. This is what's left of people's possessions from the train wreck. The depot wanted to store it in case people came back to claim it. The house's attic was near empty and became the designated storage room."

"Have many people claimed things over the years?"

"At first, yes, because the depot manager made lists of any baggage that had name tags or identification on it and tried to ship it on to its destination or back to its origin. And relatives came to claim children or visit graves. This is only a fourth of what was originally up there."

Emma moved the wooden box, about twelve-by-twelve-inches square, onto the table and opened the hinged lid for Miss Robertson to look in it.

"Ah. I think this is the right box, finally," Miss Robertson grinned at Emma. "Look at the photos and see if you recognize any of your family."

Emma reached into the box and pulled out the handful of photographs. They weren't stacked neatly and were of various sizes, the first photo upside down.

Emma turned over the first photograph and gasped as she recognized her mother.

"This is my mother! And this must be my father," Emma faltered as she stared at the young couple.

"Do you suppose that was their wedding portrait?" Miss Robertson asked as she drew near to study the couple in the studio portrait.

Emma bit her lip, trying not to cry. She didn't remember her father, and to see him for the first time made tears well up in her eyes.

Emma nodded as she touched her father's face, not able to find her voice to answer the question.

The next photo was of Robby and Emma together, seated in a large, upholstered chair. Emma was a baby and Robby a toddler. There was a distinct difference in their hair and eye coloring, even though the photo was black and white.

"This is my brother, Robby, who is two years older than me. It's funny to find this after meeting my half-brother and his son in San Antonio. There is definitely a family resemblance between the three of them."

The next photo, slightly larger than the other two, looked like it was taken when Tina was pregnant with Oliver. Her face was much rounder and Emma could see her protruding middle, even though Emma was sitting on her lap. Robby was standing beside the chair her mother was sitting in, and their father was standing behind it.

"I imagine this was taken before your father died?" Miss Robertson asked.

"Probably a few months before that fateful day. I'm so happy to have these photographs to share with my family," Emma said as she reached for Miss Robertson's hand. "Thank you so much for saving them."

"It was fate for you to come back just as I was ready to clean out the house. Now look to see what else is in the box. I'm so curious now."

There were two tintypes of older couples, but Emma didn't know who they were. They could be her grandparents but there was no writing on the backs.

"That's a new Bible," Miss Robertson pointed to the shiny leather covered book.

Emma leafed through the front of the book and saw her parents' names, and Robby's and her own.

"Well, it was new twenty years ago." Emma gently shook the book upside down, but no loose papers fell out of it.

Next were loose pages giving a history of her parents' younger years. Their wedding certificate, her father's school diploma, newspaper clippings of Emma's grandparents' passing, a couple of letters Robert wrote to Tina when they were courting. It was fascinating to get a glimpse of her parent's early marriage from this long lost box.

"Mama is going to cry with joy when I give her this box," Emma said as she got to the bottom of the box.

"There's something else in there," Miss Robertson pointed out something in the corner wrapped in a bit of calico fabric.

Emma retrieved it and felt the weight in her hand. "It's heavy."

She unwrapped the material to find a wide gold ring featuring three diamonds in a row on its top. The rest of the band was engraved with a fancy scrolling.

"Is looks like a woman's wedding band," Emma said as she slid it on her right ring finger. It was a perfect fit.

"I assume it was your relative's. Maybe a grandmother's? It looks old."

"Or my mother's ring from my father. Either way, I'm going to start wearing it now."

"Look back on your parent's wedding portrait. See if the ring is in the photo," Miss Robertson suggested.

Emma pulled the right photo out of the pile of papers and studied it. "Her left hand is showing but the photo is so small, I can't tell."

"I have a magnifying glass in my sewing basket by my rocker. Get it out and see if it helps."

Emma found the glass and moved it across the photo to zero in on the ring. She studied it a moment, handing both items to Miss Robertson for her to look at. Anna was sprawled on the woman's chest and didn't wake when Miss Robertson took the photo and glass.

"I can't move close enough to the lamp to have a good look, but I think it is the same ring. Could it be an heirloom, passed down from your Martin family?"

"What's passed down?" Carsten said as he entered the room and plopped down on a chair next to Emma.

"This ring!" Emma held out her right hand to Carsten.

"It was in a wooden box that Miss Robertson had saved from the train wreck. And this ring is on the hand of my mother in her wedding portrait!"

"Wait. There was a photo of your parents in the stuff I carried downstairs?"

"Yes! Photos, important papers and this ring!" Emma pointed to the box and then the photo still in Miss Robertson's hand.

"Take a look. I'm sure it's the same ring," Miss Robertson said as Carsten took the photo and magnifying glass from her.

"I can't believe it. What's the chance of finding this after twenty years? Unbelievable."

Anna whimpered as she started to wake. "I'll take a turn with her," Emma said as she took the child from Miss Robertson's lap.

"Thank you. She was deadweight and getting heavy," Miss Robertson said as she slowly sat forward and rolled her shoulders.

"Everything has been removed from the attic, Miss Robertson. What about the beds and dressers in the second floor bedroom? Who gets them?" Carsten asked.

"The house belongs to the city and I was told city workers will remove the furniture once I move out. The rocking chair is the only thing I'm taking with me besides my personal items."

"Then your move to your sister's home will be an easy one," Emma said, thinking it was kind of sad the only thing she would take was one item. But then she'd been an employee of the city for years and this wasn't her home.

"I rocked so many babies in that chair. Keeping it will always bring back memories of every child I helped, including you and your brother," Miss Robertson said as she pointed to Emma holding Anna.

"How does soup and sandwiches sound for our supper tonight before we retire for bed? I know you must be hungry from all your hard work, Mr. Brenner, and I know Anna needs to eat."

Emma watched Carsten's eyes widen with the announcement that Miss Robertson thought they were spending the night.

Carsten motioned for Emma to step to the side of the room as Miss Robertson walked down the hall to the kitchen.

"We can't spend the night here. She'll expect us to sleep in the same room," Carsten whispered.

"And you've already paid for two rooms in the hotel," Emma said as she rocked Anna back to sleep and thought of the situation.

They could make do in one bedroom, with one of them sleeping on the floor, but then she thought of the child in her arms.

"I wouldn't mind staying here to take care of Anna during the night, but you should go back to the hotel."

Carsten started to protest but Emma shook her head to stop him.

"There could be a telegram from Simon waiting for us, and the hotelkeeper will wonder why we didn't come back tonight too."

"True. What do you think Miss Robertson will say if you stay here and I go back to the hotel tonight?"

"Our reasons are valid. We only planned to visit the orphanage this afternoon and go back to the hotel for the night."

"Hungry," Anna murmured, even though she was still half-asleep.

"The child will be fully awake when I change her diaper in a moment. Let's get her fed and I'll retire with her upstairs."

Emma walked in front of Carsten as they headed down the hall to the bathroom, but Carsten put a hand on her shoulder to stop her.

"Don't be surprised when I kiss you before I leave for the hotel. Miss Carsten would expect that, given I'm your husband," Carsten whispered in Emma's ear.

"Thanks for warning me, Carsten. I'll look forward to it," Emma whispered back as she went into the bathroom and quietly shut the door.

Chapter 11

Carsten glanced down at the sound of the front door of the hotel shutting as he descended the carpeted steps from the hall of rooms down to the lobby. Someone else was leaving early this morning too.

He thought he wouldn't sleep well last night, worrying about Emma and Anna, but he was tired after making umpteen trips up and down the steps of the orphanage yesterday evening. His body had used different muscles than when he did his ranching duties, which normally meant hours in the saddle.

Because Emma didn't spend the night in the hotel, Carsten went in Emma's room this morning and packed her carpet bag to bring with him, thinking there would be things she'd need. He was just ready to open the outside door when he noticed the hotel clerk hold up his hand as if Carsten should stop from leaving.

"Mr. Brenner! You just received a telegram marked urgent," the clerk waved a letter in the air.

"Thank you," Carsten said as he walked to the counter and reached for the letter.

"When did this come in?" He mentioned last night to the evening clerk, that he'd be receiving one in the near future, but he didn't expect one first thing in the morning.

"The messenger was just in here. Left about the same time you came down the stairs."

Carsten walked over to one of the settees in the lobby and dropped Emma's carpet bag on it. He opened the envelope and unfolded the telegram to read the message.

To: Carsten Brenner, Glover Hotel, Austin

From: Mr. Charleston, San Antonio Ledger

Travel back immediately to get Paul. Simon Jarvis in hospital.

Carsten rubbed his face, worried about what happened to Simon and why did Simon's boss say to return for Paul.

"Problems, sir?" The clerk asked.

"Yes, a family member is in the hospital in San Antonio."

"I'm so sorry. Will you be checking out now then?"

Carsten tried to think about what to do. He could send word to the orphanage that he was going back to San Antonio, but Emma should go too in case...

Carsten didn't want to guess how Emma would handle losing her brother after just meeting him two days ago.

"Yes, I'll check out now after I retrieve the rest of our things from the rooms," Carsten called back as he took the stairs two at a time, which reminded him of his sore leg muscles.

Carsten ran over to the depot after checking out of the hotel to find out the train departures for San Antonio. There was a train in two hours. They could make that train if there was no delay in leaving the orphanage.

*

"Emma?" Carsten called out as soon as he opened the orphanage door. He didn't bother to knock, but just walked right in when he realized the door was unlocked.

"Carsten? We're in the kitchen," Emma called out and Carsten jogged down the hallway to find the group sitting at the table eating breakfast.

"Good morning, Mr. Brenner, there's coffee—"

"I'm sorry, Miss Robertson, but I don't have time for coffee this morning. Emma, we have to leave right now to catch a train back to San Antonio. I have a hired driver outside waiting to take us to the depot."

"Why?" Emma asked as she put down the spoon she'd been using to feed Anna her oatmeal.

"I got an urgent telegram from the manager of the San Antonio Ledger saying we needed to come for Paul immediately. Simon is in the hospital," Carsten said as he pulled out Emma's chair from the table.

"What happened? Is Simon going to be all right?" Emma asked in alarm.

"The telegram didn't give any more details. We barely have time to get to the depot before the next train leaves. I already checked out of the hotel and have our bags in the buggy."

Emma pulled Anna out of the highchair and handed the toddler to him.

"Please change Anna's diaper then, because she's going with us," Emma ordered Carsten in a voice that told him not to argue. "There's still one diaper on the bathroom table. I already have a bag packed for her since the three of us would be leaving for Kansas today."

"Wouldn't it be best if Anna stays with Miss Robertson while we check on Simon and Paul? Is Anna ready to travel?" Carsten asked quietly, trying not to show his confusion in his voice.

Why were they taking Anna at all, and why today?

"No, she's healing and can travel. Please get her ready, Carsten."

Carsten gave up arguing with Emma and carried Anna to the bathroom to change her. There was a reason Emma insisted Anna was going with them. He took a deep breath, worried about Anna's tender bottom, but it wasn't as red as yesterday. He gently rubbed the tube of salve on Anna's tender skin, and then stuck the salve in his vest pocket. If Anna was coming with them, so was the diaper rash treatment.

"I'm ready," Emma called out just as Carsten stepped out of the bathroom. "Wrap her in this light-weight blanket and we're ready to go. We'll buy clothes for her and more diapers when we get to San Antonio."

Why was Emma anxious to leave? It seemed to be more about worrying to get Anna out of the house than getting to her brother and nephew.

"Got your family box with you?" Carsten got the feeling they weren't coming back here for some reason.

"Yes, it's packed in the second bag," Emma lifted her other arm to show she had the box with her. "Let's go. The driver is waiting."

Carsten opened up the front door with one hand while holding Anna against his chest with the other.

"Thank you for saving our family box, Miss Robertson. My mother will be so happy to see it. We're in a hurry, so I'll just say thank you and goodbye," Emma said, picking up the bags and walking out the door, not looking back at all.

Carsten helped Emma get in the carriage, handed Anna up to her, and joined them when he got the bags stored at their feet.

"Emma, we need to hurry to the depot, but why the sudden urgency to take Anna with us?"

"Because Miss Robertson almost *sold* Anna last night," Emma choked out as she cradled Anna to her chest.

Carsten stared at Emma, sure he'd heard her wrong, but the tears in Emma's eyes showed she was serious.

"What happened?" Carsten said as he stroked Anna's silky hair. Emma must have cut her singed hair because it was all one length now, rather than longer on one side.

"This *slimy* middle-aged man came to the door just as we were about to retire for bed. He'd heard Miss Robertson had a new orphan and wanted to *buy* her, like he did her *last* child in her care."

"She said it been adopted! Are you *sure*?" Carsten asked, not believing the older woman could do that to children in her care.

"Miss Robertson asked if she'd get the same price as the last girl he bought!"

Carsten blew out a breath, trying to comprehend buying a child, but he knew it happened.

"I pushed the man out the door telling him my husband and I had already adopted the child and she wasn't for sale."

Carsten rubbed a hand over his face. He couldn't disagree with Emma's actions but now they had Anna to take care of.

"What did Miss Robertson say then?"

"She admitted doing it to clear the way for her to retire, and that she needed the money."

"I can't believe someone who spent years running an orphanage would to that, especially since she could have moved the child to the new orphanage."

Emma let out a long breath. "Her health was giving her problems, and she was ready to quit. She favored her right knee when she walked."

"What are we going to do with Anna?"

Emma looked down at the child nestled against her chest and sighed.

"Anna keeps calling me Mama. And I do feel obligated to take care of her, like Miss Robertson took care of me and Robby. But…"

"But what?" Carsten asked, already guessing what the answer would be.

"She deserves a good home. I need a husband and home to keep her."

"You would make a good mother, Emma," Carsten told her as he moved his arm and wrapped it around her shoulders.

"And you'd make a good father, Carsten. We've talked about courting. Is Anna the reason to skip that step and marry?"

"Yes, but don't I get the privilege of asking for your hand in marriage first?" Carsten asked before leaning over and kissing the side of Emma's head.

He'd already made up his mind after the first leg of their trip together that he'd ask her father for his blessing when they arrived home. Then Emma and her mother would have time to plan for their wedding at their church.

"What about Anna though? I don't think Miss Robertson nor the storekeeper who brought her to the orphanage filed a report with police but we're leaving town with a child we assume is abandoned. We should file for her adoption in Austin before we leave town, but we don't have time today. I suppose we could stop at city hall on the way back to Kansas?" Emma asked.

"Or we wait until we get home and have Lyle Elison file papers for us," Carsten suggested as he hugged Emma closer. His dream of a wife and family living with him on the Cross C Ranch was going to come true sooner than he thought, but he was excited about it now.

They were pulling up to the depot and his mind switched to getting his new family on the train to San Antonio.

Emma smiled up at Carsten and his heart melted as Emma's love for him and Anna shined in her eyes.

Chapter 12

Emma's mind switched for a time to worrying about Simon and Paul as soon as they were settled on the train to San Antonio.

But then her thoughts went to buying their little girl clothes and bringing her home to Kansas.

Now Emma's focus was back on Simon and Paul. They arrived at the newspaper office to find out exactly where Simon and Paul were, but then they had to sit ten minutes waiting for Mr. Charleston to see them. Her patience was stretched thin when he finally ushered them into his office.

Mr. Charleston had given them directions to the hospital and babysitters, but then stopped them before they left the room.

"Before you leave, I need to tell you one more thing," Mr. Charleston said, although he wouldn't meet Emma's eyes. "When Simon is discharged from the hospital, he cannot return here. His employment has been terminated, which also includes his living upstairs."

"How can you fire Simon for the accident? Hasn't he worked here for years?" Emma was appalled by Mr. Charleston's callous tone. "Did he do something wrong or is it an excuse to get rid of him?"

Mr. Charleston looked up at Emma but stalled before answering.

"Ever since Simon's wife died, it's been hard for him to do his job. I didn't mind that he asked for time off to visit his family in Kansas. But then his carelessness caused the press to break in the next hour. And it isn't the first mistake I've had to overlook in the past months."

"But you can't just take away his job and housing. He needs both more than ever," Emma chortled back her rage.

"No, Simon needs his *family*. He told me about you and your big family in Kansas, who are his relations he didn't know about. What Simon needs is his family, not this job or the one room upstairs he calls home. *Please.* Clean out his meager belongings upstairs. Check him out of the hospital, get Paul from his babysitter, and take them back to Kansas with you."

"Before we do that, I'll collect any wages he's due from you," Emma stated as she held out her hand and tapped her foot.

"I think that will go to the press repair," Mr. Charleston said as he crossed his arms.

"The man is now crippled and without a job. Did you pay his hospital bill? Pay the babysitter for the extra day she took care of Paul?"

Silence hung in the air as Emma waited for Mr. Charleston to answer.

"I'll pay the hospital bill. One of the other workers said they had just spilled oil on the floor, which *might* have caused Simon to fall," the man relented.

"And his wages due up to the accident. Please, Mr. Charleston. You know he's had a rough life. He doesn't need for you to injure his pride too by leaving him penniless."

"I paid for his wife's funeral after she committed suicide. He's been paying me back a little each week. But I'll consider it paid up to help him out."

"Suicide?" Emma gasped. "Laura killed herself?"

"He didn't tell you? She drank two bottles of laudanum and never woke up."

"No, Simon said he came home one day to find she'd passed, but we didn't press him for information."

That news took the wind out of Emma's lungs.

"It's all right, Emma. We'll take Paul and Simon back to Kansas, if he wants to go," Carsten added.

Now they'd have an injured man and two youngsters to take care of. But they could do it. Emma rose, held out her hand to Mr. Charleston and waited for him to reluctantly grasp it.

"Thank you for your help, Mr. Charleston. We'll be back to clean out Simon's room once we check on Simon and pick up Paul. How do we get into his home?"

"Go up the outside staircase from the back alley to reach the upper set of rooms. Simon should have a door key for his room."

Emma cringed when Carsten sighed, knowing what he was thinking when hearing the location of Simon's room. Carsten would have to carry everything down a flight of steps like he did at the orphanage.

*

Emma bit her tongue to keep from crying when she saw Simon, lying on his back in the hospital bed, pale and deathly still. His forehead and nose were swollen with numerous small cuts on his face. His eyes were swollen shut. But his worst injuries were his two broken arms. His left arm had a plaster cast from his hand to his elbow, with the tips of his bruised fingers showing. His right arm was bent at the elbow with a cast from his fingers to his shoulder. There were splints on three of his fingers that must be broken too.

"How long does Mr. Jarvis need to stay in the hospital?" Carsten asked the doctor who had entered the room with him.

"If Mr. Jarvis has someone to take care of him, he can leave. There's not much else we can do for him at this point. His face will heal in time. The plaster casts can come off in six weeks, and then we'll see if there is permanent damage. Luckily, the bones didn't break through the skin."

"Bones? How many breaks does the poor man have?" Carsten asked.

It was good that Carsten was with her, because she couldn't think straight to ask questions.

"In simple terms, he broke the lower forearm bone in his left arm. But in his right, he broke both forearm bones, and his humerus bone right below where it connects to his shoulder. That break could easily take three months to heal."

Emma put a hand over her mouth, trying her best not to heave her stomach contents. Carsten shifted Anna to his right side and rubbed his left hand along the back of Emma's neck.

"Take a deep breath, Emma. He's going to be all right," Carsten stated, but he didn't sound too sure of his words.

"Can he stay here another night? We need to find his son and get hotel rooms for all of us," Carsten asked the doctor.

"Find his son?"

"Mr. Jarvis' six-month-old son, Paul, is staying with a babysitter, but we need to find the woman's home and pick him up."

"Jarvis' employee said he wasn't married and had no one to contact except his sister in Austin, which he'd sent a telegram to. I didn't know he had a baby."

"My brother's wife died four months ago," Emma explained to the doctor.

"A sad situation then. I'm glad you live in Austin. I assume he can live with you for the next two or three months?"

"Actually, we live in Kansas and stopped to see Austin on our way home after visiting him. His employer sent a telegram to our hotel and caught us before we left."

Carsten's simple explanation was all the doctor needed to know.

"How long do we need to stay in San Antonio before he can travel?" Carsten asked next.

"I'd give him three or four days at least. Then maybe travel part way and stop again for another day if need be.

"Mr. Jarvis is heavily medicated for the pain and should sleep through the night. I suggest you pick up your nephew now and get a good night's sleep. Come back after lunch tomorrow and we'll release him to you. That will give us time to ease up on his medication and be sure he's able to leave," the doctor said.

"Thank you, doctor. We appreciate all your help. We'll see you tomorrow," Carsten said before gently taking Emma's elbow to guide her out of the room and out of the hospital.

Emma took several deep breaths once they were out of the building, but she couldn't help the tears running down her cheeks.

"Oh, Carsten. He looks terrible, and he has to be in so much pain!"

"I know. And he has a long recovery ahead of him. I hope his arms heal, because if they don't, he's going to be crippled for life."

Emma turned to Carsten and slipped her arms around his middle, soaking up his strength to calm her down.

"Mama," Anna patted the top of Emma's head, causing her to feel better, but to remind her of their other responsibilities.

"Thank you, Anna. I need your hug too." Emma wiped her eyes and held out her arms to Anna, who slipped from Carsten's arms into hers. Emma gave her a gentle hug, instantly feeling better.

"Ready to take charge of another baby?" Carsten said, trying to slip a little lightness in his tone.

"Sure. This only makes two children for us to take care of," Emma said as she took a deep breath and straightened her shoulders. "Your adoptive parents instantly had to take charge of six children in one afternoon."

"That's the right attitude, Emma. Let's find Paul."

*

"I can't believe Simon would leave Paul with that woman. The place was *filthy*, she was ignoring his crying as he lay in that *dirty* bed and—"

"And now Paul is safe with us, Carsten," Emma said to calm Carsten down. They had just left the babysitter's house and now Carsten was venting his anger.

The woman wasn't going to let Emma take Paul until Carsten bribed her with money. That changed her mind right quick.

"He probably has hair lice," Carsten growled.

"I'll give him a good bath when we get back to the hotel."

"He's hungry!"

"Yes, as are the *rest* of us, Carsten."

"We forgot to get Simon's key."

Oh, shoot. So much for clean clothes for Paul then.

And that's how their conversation went for the three-block walk back to their hotel, going from bickering to silence and back.

Emma stopped at the front desk of the hotel while Carsten continued stomping up the stairs with Anna in his arms.

"Could you ask the dining room to bring up a large plate of sandwiches, a pot of coffee, and a large pitcher of warm milk to room three, please?" Emma asked sweetly, knowing if she spoke how she felt, the clerk would ask her to go to the dining room herself.

"Yes, ma'am," the clerk said, after watching Carsten storm up the steps. He hesitated a moment and then asked, "rough day?"

Emma decided to be truthful, because they were going to be in this hotel for several days.

"Yes, it has been a *horrible* day. We're from out of town and got a telegram that my brother was in an accident. We traveled here immediately and found him in the hospital, badly bruised with *both* arms broken. My brother is a *widower*, and when we went to pick up his *baby* from the person who was taking care of him, we were *appalled* by the lack of care he was given," Emma told the man, while trying to comfort a crying, whining Paul. She might have been a little dramatic with her explanation, but she needed all the sympathy and help they could get. Emma was afraid the man would be listening to Paul and Anna cry off and on all night.

"Is this the poor little guy?" the clerk asked.

"Yes, this is Paul. He's confused because he's not with his daddy, and he's so hungry and tired."

"I'll get food and milk up to your room right away. Do you need a tin tub and hot water to bathe the child too?"

"Oh, that would be so much help. I'm sure he'd sleep better after a warm bath and a full tummy. Thank you so much, Mr. —"

"Mr. Jeffries, at your service, Mrs. Brenner."

And to think they came to Texas to see two graves and a cattle ranch.

Chapter 13

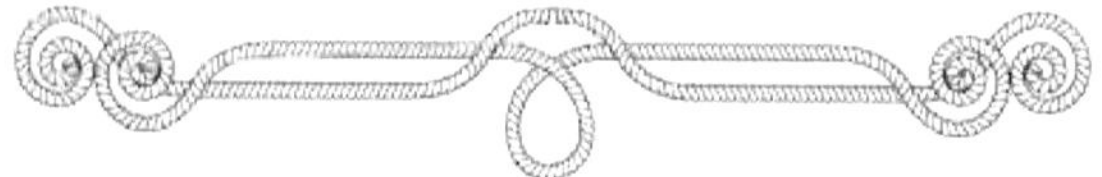

"I'm sorry I've been a bad pretend husband and father this evening," Carsten softly apologized to Emma, who was lying beside him in bed. Carsten tried to shift Anna off his chest again, but she crawled right back up, wanting to keep her head on his beating heart.

They had given up putting the children in the furnished crib for Anna and basket for Paul because they cried the minute they were moved.

Carsten turned his head to see if Emma was still awake, and she was, still gently running her fingers up and down Paul's tiny back.

"It's okay. It's been a trying day for all four of us. And sometimes a typical day for a real couple with their own young children," Emma replied as she turned her head to face him.

Emma was so pretty lying there, her hair in a night braid over her shoulder, a child on her chest.

Love for this woman hit him in the heart as hard as Anna had kicked him in the chin when he was trying to give the tyke a bath. Both hurt but felt good at the same time.

"Let's get married for real, Emma. As much as I thought I hated this day, I loved doing it with you."

"Is that love or exhaustion talking now, Carsten?" Emma chuckled.

"Maybe both?" Carsten said, and then stayed silent a minute to see if she'd agree to marry him.

"Can we wait to marry when we get home? I'd like our family to witness it," Emma said as she reached her left hand to find his right hand on the bed between them.

"I'd like that. Thanks for letting me escort you on your trip, Emma. I've always liked you, but this gave us a test to prove we can have a good marriage."

"And to think I was hoping for courtship, flowers, and chocolates," Emma said dramatically. "Instead I received a burned toddler from a saloon, an injured brother I didn't know existed, and his baby who really did have head lice," Emma sighed.

"I was *joking* when I said Paul had head lice. I never dreamed it would be true."

"Not even after seeing the filth in that house?"

"Good point."

Emma combed Paul's hair several times while Carsten held a lamp over the child's head to look for any lice or eggs. She had only found three but getting rid of those would save the rest of them from getting lice too.

It had been a long evening. Asking the hotel clerk to send food to their room was a godsend, even if it was simple ham and cheese sandwiches. They were filling, and that's what their empty stomachs needed.

"What all do we have to do in the morning before we go to the hospital?"

Carsten's mind was jumbled with thoughts and questions, but he knew Emma would have an organized list in her head.

"Breakfast first. I want biscuits and gravy, a poached egg, and bacon."

Carsten mentally groaned at the thought of an egg on Emma's plate, but if the children would eat them, he'd have to learn how to cook them and endure the smell.

"Then we need to shop for clothing. For each child, and for Simon."

"Don't you think Simon would have clothes in his room? We just need to get his key and retrieve them."

"All three times we've seen Simon, his clothes have been threadbare and patched. And he lost his shirt, literally, when he fell onto the press."

"Paul's clothes are tight now, and not going to fit at all once he's properly fed."

"And Anna needs everything from drawers to shoes," Carsten guessed.

"Along with a pretty dress, a traveling bonnet and coat, and a doll for her to clutch instead of you all the time."

"But I like her clutching me," Carsten teased Emma, "but, if she had a dolly, then I guess you could be wrapped in my arms instead."

"Ha! Remember we have Paul to take care of too. Simon won't be able to hold his son for weeks."

"What a sad thought. I'm glad we're here for him, Emma. I can't imagine having something like that happen to me and not have family to help."

"I am too. Thank you so much for all you are doing for all of them, and me."

"Nothing but the best for my pretend wife, Mrs. Brenner," Carsten chuckled.

"And while at the store we need books, not only for the children, but to read to Simon. He'll be in a lot of pain for a while, but he's going to be bored out of his mind after he catches up on his sleep."

"I'm glad Grandpa Isaac gave us extra money for our trip. He said you always need to carry plenty of money on trips for emergencies. I doubt he thought it would be used for clothing, hotel, and train fare for three extra people though."

"Both sets of our grandparents will be enthusiastic with adding new members to our families."

"And us marrying." Carsten moved their clasped hands to his mouth and kissed Emma's hand. "We both had rough starts in life but were given a second chance being adopted into wonderful, caring families."

"And we'll do the same for the three in our care," Emma assured him.

*

"Now I wish we had one of those trunks I hauled from the attic of the orphanage," Carsten said as he carried the multiple wrapped packages out of the mercantile.

The first thing Emma did when they walked into the store was pick out a soft cloth doll that she handed each child to hold. Then she picked out a wicker buggy and moved the children, with their new toy, into the buggy. She instructed the store clerk to start her bill with those items, and then instructed Carsten to go outside with the buggy and children.

That allowed Emma to have free hands and a focused mind to go through the stacks of clothing to pick out what each person needed. And to keep the clerk and other customers from seeing the children too. Everyone gasped when they saw Anna's burned skin and hair. Carsten was glad Emma had bought a large bonnet for Anna which shielded the side of her face and put it on the girl as soon as they walked out the door of the mercantile.

"Only one trunk? We don't know yet what all Simon has to bring with him to Kansas."

"And to think I have to haul it all downstairs," Carsten groaned.

"You'll manage. I bet the furniture stays with the room, and he'll have few personal belongings. Neither he nor his wife would have any family items as keepsakes since they grew up in an orphanage."

"Any other stops before we go back to the hotel for lunch?" Carsten asked as he looked up and down the street to read the store front signs.

"We need to go across the street to the bookstore. I'll stay outside with the children while you shop this time," Emma said as they looked both directions before crossing the street.

"What do I need to buy?"

"Pictures books for the children and whatever you want to read to Simon. Nothing that would scare the children though. They'll be in Simon's room part of the time."

Carsten had booked two rooms, one beside the other and across from the bathroom. Emma and the children would stay and sleep in one room when Simon needed to be alone. Carsten would help Simon with his toilet needs and sleep whenever and wherever he could.

He didn't spend much time in the bookstore, knowing the children were getting hungry for lunch. But after stacking his choices on the counter, he went back to the children's section again for an alphabet book. It was for sentimental reasons because Anna wasn't two years old yet, but his father Marcus had taken an alphabet book with him to Fort Wallace when he adopted Molly and Moses.

Carsten was filled with pride when he walked out the door. He'd bought books for his little girl.

*

"Simon? Simon, please talk to us. Your son needs to hear your voice," Emma pleaded with Simon when they arrived at the hospital after lunch. Her brother remained laying on his side in the bed, facing the wall.

Emma insisted she and the children come with Carsten to get Simon, but Carsten wasn't sure it was a good idea now. Simon was in pain and his discolored face looked scary to the children. And Simon wouldn't look at Paul, which worried Carsten.

Was Simon still drugged, or feeling so downtrodden he didn't want to live? Laura's suicide had to be on his mind as pain wracked his body.

Carsten would be sure any pain medicine for Simon wouldn't be left in his room unattended, and also kept out of Anna's reach for that matter. Anna was turning into a climber as she felt better. His mother, Sarah, would have to "baby-proof" the ranch house when they returned home and moved in with his parents for a while.

"Who that?" Anna asked as she pointed a finger at Simon. "Hurt like me?"

Simon's fatherly instincts made him look over his shoulder when a child spoke of being hurt.

"Anna, this is your Uncle Simon. His face was hurt too but will heal like yours will. But he also hurt his arms. Do you see they are wrapped in plaster bandages?"

"Touch?" Anna asked as she leaned out of Carsten's arms, wanting to touch his arms.

"Not yet, but I bet you can when we get him back to the hotel," Emma promised Anna.

Simon turned back to the wall after glancing at Anna. "Gathering more wounded, Emma?"

"Carsten's and my family are known for that. We added Anna to our family this week. She was in a fire in Austin and orphaned recently. She'll be traveling with us to Kansas, along with you and Paul," Emma said matter-of-factly.

"You can take Paul because I don't plan to live long enough to get to Kansas."

Emma stared at Simon, either stunned at his implication, or worried he was that injured.

"Good, glad to see you're here to pick up your brother, Mrs. Brenner," the doctor interrupted them as he walked in the door.

"Here's his pain medication, but he should be able to do without it in a day or two. Ice and cold cloths on his face will help the swelling. I'd suggest keeping his right arm in a sling until that cast comes off. He can toss the left arm sling anytime he's comfortable without it."

As the doctor talked he gently pulled Simon to an upright position, swung his legs off the bed, and feet onto the floor.

"Mr. Jarvis has already been in and out of bed a few times, so he knows how to balance with his arms being braced in place.

"Any questions?" the doctor continued as he glanced at all the faces in the room.

"If not, have your doctor in Kansas check his arms when you get home. Have him take off the casts in six weeks. Take care now."

"Uh, now what?" A shocked Simon looked at Emma and then Carsten after the doctor's rapid fire talk and swift departure.

"Don't worry, Simon. You're now in your big sister's care," Carsten answered with a grin.

Before Simon could protest, Emma sat Paul on his knee, while holding him in place. Paul studied his father's face, ready to cry until Simon said, "I missed you, Paul. Have you been a good boy for your Aunt Emma?"

Carsten watched as both Paul's and Emma's faces brightened into smiles. It would be a tough week, but everyone would improve in body and spirit with the help of Emma, his pretend, but also future wife.

Chapter 14

"Have you ever had a dog?" Emma asked Simon as they sat in his room, getting to know each other. Simon slept almost all day yesterday, but today he was awake and restless. All he could do was lay on his back, his arms across his chest, and think about his predicament.

Carsten was in the other room, sleeping, after being up with Simon part of the night. Last Emma looked, Paul was peacefully sleeping by himself in the basket.

Emma was sitting in a rocker by Simon's bed with Anna quietly dozing in her arms, asking questions about his past and telling him about hers. The time they spent talking and getting to know each other was precious, and Emma meant to make the most of Simon's confinement.

"No. I was in an orphanage, and I couldn't have one in my room upstairs in the newspaper building," Simon scoffed.

Emma ignored his bad mood but continued talking.

"There was a huge brown mutt that hung out at our orphanage. His name was Samson, and I think he was a mastiff. When Leif and Mama claimed us at the orphanage, Samson followed us out of town to the ranch cabin we stayed at a few days while Mama recovered.

"That dog followed us from Texas to Kansas behind our wagon and the cattle on the drive.

"I don't remember Samson at that time since I was so young, but Leif said the dog only liked cooked meat. Samson must have eaten scraps from around town instead of hunting. He'd catch wild animals, rabbits, badgers, whatever, but then he'd bring it back to the camp for Mama to cook instead of just eating it after he caught it. Samson caught so much game he furnished the family with food to eat."

"Did the dog survive the trip?" Simon asked, now interested in her story.

"Yep. I was ten when Samson slinked off and died. Leif found him by the old chuckwagon the Hamners always used for cattle drives."

"Mama, bed," Anna said as she slid off Emma's lap and waited for Emma to get out of the rocker and lift her onto Simon's bed.

"Careful of Uncle Simon's arms, Sweetie."

The child crawled across the bed to lay her head next to Simon's. Emma hoped Anna would close her eyes and go back to sleep.

"Why does she already call you Mama? It seems like she's settled into life with you and Carsten with ease."

"I was told I look like her mother, Raven. The woman worked in the saloon that burned down in Austin. I think it's helped with Anna's anxieties, so I never corrected Anna since the first time she called me that," Emma shrugged as she sat down again.

"Did you ever think of taking her to the new orphanage in Austin instead of adopting her?"

"No, because I knew it was fate that put me in that place and time to raise her. It has to do with my upbringing, but as soon as I saw Anna, hurt, burned, and needing love, it just hit me that I should take her, even if Carsten weren't in the picture."

"I thought of giving Paul up for adoption after Laura died. The grief and trying to figure out what to do with him were overwhelming," Simon hoarsely whispered.

"I can understand that," Emma said, then thought about what they hadn't talked about yet.

"Simon, Carsten went over to your room yesterday."

Simon grimaced, and Emma didn't know if it was from his physical pain or shame at what was in his room, which was hardly anything. Carsten fit all of Simon and Paul's belongings worth keeping into one carpetbag. There wasn't a single photograph, book, or toy in the room.

"I assume he was there for a change of clothes for us?"

Emma hesitated a minute and decided it was best to tell Simon the facts.

"When we arrived at the newspaper to find where you were, Mr. Charleston said we should clean out your room, as you were no longer employed there," Emma stated and braced herself for his shock.

"*What!* He *fired* me? *Why*! Yes, the newspaper edition didn't get out that night, but it wasn't my fault! I was pushed into the press!"

"Mr. Charleston never mentioned that. He thought you slipped on something wet on the floor," Emma gasped at the thought of someone trying to hurt her brother on purpose.

"Did you tell anyone after the accident? Report it to the police?" Emma's mind raced with questions.

"No use to. A man has harassed me since I started working there. Friend of my late father, George Jarvis, still thought Robert Martin deserved to be shot, and Robert's son continued to pay for his sins. I imagine he gave the shove that caused me to fall. I bet he was hoping I'd lose my arms instead of just my job."

Emma sat stunned as she watched the emotions displayed on her brother's bruised face. Why did people want to hurt another person? How could they justify their mean actions?

"Why didn't you move to another town when you were of age? Change your name?"

"Why bother? Back luck would follow me," Simon sighed and turned his face toward Anna when he felt the little girl touch his face.

Emma didn't bother picking up Anna because Simon and Anna needed each other in their own way. Anna gently ran her index finger across

Simon's cuts and bruises and then moved her finger to touch the sores on her face.

"I hope she isn't scarred for life," Simon choked out, and Emma was glad he was thinking about someone else besides himself.

"She'll grow into a beautiful woman, no matter what," Emma stated firmly.

Simon turned his face toward Emma and slightly smiled for the first time since leaving the hospital.

"She will, huh? Is that according to her mother?"

"Yes. And as a sister and an aunt, I want to be sure you and Paul have a better life too. Please travel to Kansas with us. Start over by living with our family."

"Should I change our name too to fit in?"

"Martin is your birthright to use just as it is for Robby and Oliver."

"Your mother didn't change their last name? You said Leif adopted you. Didn't he adopt your brothers?"

"Leif adopted all of us, but Mama wanted her sons to remember their father. They've always used Martin for their surname. Mama changed my name to Hamner because I called Leif my papa from the very first time I met him."

"If Paul and I move to Kansas and change our last name to Martin, do we get a dog too?" Simon asked as a joke.

"Dog?" Anna pushed her hand on Simon's shoulder to sit up and look at Emma.

"Yes, all three of you can have a dog. Even better, a puppy, because I know one of the Cross C ranch dogs had puppies right before we left on our trip," Emma assured them.

"Will it be all right to move in with Carsten's parents until I get my casts off, get a job, and a place to live?" Simon asked with worry.

"Absolutely. The Cross C Ranch and Clear Creek community is the perfect place to start your lives over," Emma assured Simon.

*

"You know this is embarrassing to be spoon-fed in public," Simon grumbled as they sat in the hotel dining room for their noon meal.

"Especially when you make a face and whine," Emma teased him.

They all needed a change of scenery from their hotel room, and Simon was finally comfortable to sit upright after lying in bed for three days. Carsten said Simon's chest was also bruised from the fall, but Simon never mentioned it to Emma, so she didn't bring it up.

Now Emma held Paul in her lap with one hand while spooning soft food into the baby's mouth. Anna sat to her right in a highchair, playing with her food as much as eating it. The toddler needed to learn how to use a spoon, but that lesson would wait until they returned home.

"At least you're eating a good roast beef meal instead of runny potatoes like Paul's stuck with," Carsten teased Simon as he held a forkful of the tasty meat up for Simon to pick off the fork with his lips and tongue.

"True. When are we leaving for Kansas? I'm ready to travel," Simon said after swallowing his food.

Emma raised her eyebrows at Simon after glancing at Carsten. Simon hadn't agreed to leave San Antonio until now.

"Whenever you feel up to it," Carsten said, not questioning if Simon was ready for the uncomfortable train ride yet.

Emma cut the right side seam and sleeve of Simon's old shirts to get the material around

Simon's right arm when they were out in public. He wouldn't be able to wear his vest and jacket when they traveled, but it was May and he wouldn't need them for warmth.

All they had to do was telegraph their family they were on their way home and get on the train.

Last night, while they were alone, Carsten and Emma penned the wording of the telegram they'd send to announce Simon's presence.

Met Emma's half-brother, Simon Jarvis Martin, in San Antonio. Injured widower with baby traveling home with us.

Although their parents would be shocked by the news, they'd be open to Simon and Paul moving to Clear Creek.

"What's the plan when we get to Kansas?" Simon asked without looking up from his plate.

Emma couldn't help smiling at Carsten because they'd finalized their future last night.

"I'll be back to ranching with my father and grandfather. Emma will be taking care of our daughter, nephew, and you, until you can ride a horse and chase cattle," Carsten told Simon.

"Ranching will not be my profession if I can help it. I'm hoping the town's new newspaper will be my future," Simon said with a hint of worry in his voice.

"Sounds like a good plan. Emma and I will live in the ranch house until our home is built. You and Paul can stay with us or move into town when you're healed. I'm sure my sisters will fight over who gets to take care of Paul while you're at work."

"I still can't believe I have brothers and siblings-in-law in Kansas."

"You'll be claimed by our parents and grandparents too. Just smile and accept it," Emma told Simon as she spooned food into Paul's waiting mouth.

Chapter 15

"Oh, beans," Simon murmured when he looked out the passenger car window. Carsten looked out the window, too, as the engine's brakes slowed the train to a halt in front of the Clear Creek depot platform.

Simon turned to Carsten and asked, "has the whole town turned out to lynch me as soon as I get off the train?"

"Nope, just family members ready to meet you and Paul. All the tall blond people are the Hamner clan, except for the dark-haired Tina and Oliver, who look like Emma. Can you see Robby standing behind Emma's mother?"

Well, I'll be. We do look alike," Simon exclaimed as he stared at the man who was his half-brother.

The other half of the crowd is my Brenner family. My parents, one brother, three sisters, and their families. I don't see Asher and Beckett here, though. I wonder if they are home on the ranch, or not back from their trips yet?"

"Who is standing beside Moses, Carsten? The woman is holding a baby, and there's an older gentleman I don't know," Emma asked as she craned her neck to see the crowd.

"Don't know. Wouldn't it be funny if Moses married and brought extra family home from his trip to western Kansas last month?" Carsten asked as he studied the new people.

"Mama's moved forward, ready to meet you, Simon," Emma pointed to her mother, who indeed had moved close to the passenger cars, searching the windows for them.

"There! She's seen us! Wave at your Grandma Tina, Anna," Emma said as she gently picked up Anna's left hand and placed it against the window glass.

"Oh, my gosh! Did you see how wide your mother's eyes widened when she saw Anna on your lap?" Carsten chuckled. This was going to be a fun reunion.

"Our turn to get off. Ready, Simon?" Carsten said as he stood and pulled the children's satchel off the top rack. When traveling with children in diapers, the bag was the most essential item to keep with them.

"I'll take Anna, Emma, if you want to take Paul. He's lighter and easier for you to carry down the steps," Carsten suggested.

"Okay, let's go. Be ready for hugs, Simon, Paul, and Anna. You're about to meet your family," Emma said and smiled up at Carsten. "Think we'll surprise them, Carsten?"

"The way our happy mothers are acting, I think they figured it out," Carsten noted. Tina and his mother had their arms wrapped around each other's waist, and both were grinning ear to ear.

Emma carefully descended the car steps and waited for Simon to step down to join her before walking to their mothers. Simon's face was still covered with bruises, but they were more yellow than bright purple. Both arms were still in slings as it was the least painful way to support them.

Carsten stood at the top of the steps a second to wave at his family. He couldn't help but grin widely when Moses pointed at the baby in his arms and then pointing to Carsten and Anna. It looks like they both adopted a child on their trips.

Carsten stepped down to join Emma, Simon, and their parents.

"Mama, I'd like you to meet Simon Jarvis Martin and his son, Paul. George Jarvis shot his wife, Maria, and Papa when Simon was only three days old.

"I met them in San Antonio when we went to find Papa's grave and then visited the newspaper where Simon worked. He was planning to visit Clear Creek, but after his accident I convinced him this would be a good place to start over with his family."

Carsten watched Tina absorb the news with dignity. Simon's features proved she now knew her first husband cheated on her, but she didn't blame Simon for it.

"It's so nice to meet you, Simon. I'm so glad you're here."

"Thank you, Mrs. Hamner. I appreciate you accepting my presence. I didn't know if I should come, but Emma insisted you wouldn't hold the past against me," Simon said, and then lifted his arm splints. "I was in an accident and needed help taking care of my son for a while. Emma and Carsten assured me I'd be accepted here."

"They are right. The past is in the past, and you have family here in Clear Creek," Tina said as she turned and waved the Hamner family toward them.

"I'd like you to meet your brothers, Robby, a four-years-older version of yourself, and Oliver, who would be a few months younger than you. This is my husband, Leif, and our sons, Finn and Saul."

All the men nodded to Simon since he couldn't shake their hands. "Nice to meet you. I thought I was alone in the world until Emma walked into my workplace and declared I was her brother," Simon said nervously.

"Emma may be a petite female, but she's always been in charge of us four brothers," Robby told Simon. "Welcome to the family."

"Thank you. I grew up in an orphanage and never had the luxury of family."

"How old is your son?" Tina asked as she reached to take Paul out of Emma's arms.

"Paul just turned six months last week, but it's hard to tell since he's on the small side. I figured out he, uh, didn't have the best caretaker while I was at work."

"The telegram Carsten sent said you are a widower. I'm sorry you lost your wife. You've had a rough year," Tina said as she rocked Paul, who stared at Leif behind her. Paul had a lot of laps to sit on in his future.

"My wife, Laura, died when Paul was six weeks old. Emma convinced me I could start over here," Simon said tentatively.

"Many of us faced hard times and found a better life in Clear Creek. We'll do our best to help you and Paul any way we can," Tina said, and Leif nodded to confirm her offer.

"Now that we've met Simon and Paul, who is this little one you're holding, Carsten?" Carsten's ma, Sarah, asked as his parents moved forward.

"This is Anna," Emma told them. "After meeting Simon, we went on to Austin to visit the cemetery. We located the Bailey Saloon where you were for a time, Mama, but the place had burned down days before.

"Then we found the orphanage where Robby and I stayed, and the woman who took care of us was still there! Miss Robertson is retiring and couldn't take the child brought to her from the fire—"

"You married and adopted a child? That's wonderful! Congratulations!" Carsten's mother gushed as she reached for Anna.

"Careful, Ma. Anna was in a fire recently and still has burned skin on her right side," Carsten said as he turned Anna around so his parents could see her injuries. "She'll heal though and be fine."

"Yes, she will," Sarah said as she cuddled the child in her arms. "Hello, Anna. I'm your grandma Sarah."

"When and where did you get married?" Leif spoke for the first time since their arrival. Was he upset Carsten hadn't asked him for Emma's hand in marriage?

"Actually, we aren't, yet," Carsten admitted.

"You and Emma aren't married?" Simon asked with surprise. "You introduced yourself that way when we met."

"No, you just assumed our status, and we never corrected you, nor did we tell Miss Robertson the truth. It made things easier for the children's care if people considered us married," Carsten answered.

"What are your plans now?" Carsten's father, Marcus, asked.

"We plan to marry and live on the ranch. Grandpa Isaac offered me a house, but can we stay at the main house with you until we've built our place?"

"We have plenty of room for all of you. Simon, you, and Paul, too. Even though Moses brought a bride, a daughter, and his *uncle* home from western Kansas after you left on your trip," Sarah said as she reached to pull the unfamiliar woman to her side.

"Your *uncle,* Moses? You found family on your trip?" Carsten wasn't the only one with surprises, after all.

Moses came forward with the new people. "This is John Geller, my father's older brother. And my wife, Faith, who is John's adopted daughter. This special little girl is Sophie Mae Brenner. The graveyard where my parents were buried was in their ranch pasture," Moses said as he stroked the child's head.

"Sounds like we have a lot of catching up to do," Carsten said. Are you all staying at the main house too?"

"Yep, and Ma's thrilled with having a baby in the house again."

"And now I bring in two more," Carsten said, shaking his head at the irony of them adopting children as their sisters did.

"Are Asher and Beckett home yet?" Carsten turned to ask his father.

"No, I guess in the commotion of meeting your new family, we forgot they should have been with you. Where are they?"

"They split away from us the first day. Asher and Alva went to Chicago to tour the World's Fair, and Beckett and Greta went to Louisville to see the Kentucky Derby. I assumed they beat us home since we were delayed."

"No telegram from them, but I'll check before we go back to the ranch today," Marcus said as he looked back at the depot.

Was there too much to see to get back in the planned ten days, or did they run into trouble? The family wouldn't know until they returned or sent a telegram.

"We're here! What do you need?" Pastor Reagan raised his voice as he and his wife, Kaitlyn, rushed up to the family.

"Slow down, Pastor, you're out of breath. What's wrong?" Marcus asked as he looked around the crowd.

"Tim and Tom ran into our house and said we were needed right away at the depot."

Carsten looked down at his grinning six-year-old nephews. "What are you up to, boys?"

"Mama and Aunt Maggie said to get the preacher, so we did," said Tom, or maybe it was Tim who spoke. They were identical and hard to tell apart.

"Oh, Deuteronomy, boys. I about had a heart attack when you came charging in the house screaming I needed to get to the depot pronto," Pastor wheezed out as he tried to catch his breath.

"Maggie, Molly. Why did the preacher need to join us right now?" Carsten asked as his sisters walked up to join the inner circle surrounding him and Emma.

"Pastor Reagan married Peter and me, and Molly and Tobin, in this same spot by the depot when we adopted our children," Maggie answered Carsten.

"Since you've adopted a child, and both of your families are gathered here now, it seems like the proper place and time for your wedding," Molly smiled sweetly. "I'm sorry, Pastor, that the boys scared you, but they got you here."

"Got some flowers!" Maisie announced as she trotted up to Emma and handed her a handful of pink and white peony blossoms.

"You got the pastor and the flowers. What else do you need?" Moses laughed as he asked Carsten, knowing how their sisters could plan anything at a moment's notice.

"How about a father's blessing, a proposal for the bride-to-be, and a ring?" Carsten chortled, taken by surprise by his siblings' actions.

"You got my blessing," Leif announced.

"I'm saying yes, Carsten," Emma smiled up at Carsten, "and my ring is already on my left hand. But before we marry, I need to give something to Mama."

Everyone watched as Emma pulled off her right glove and held out her hand to show her mother the ring on her finger.

"Mama, was this your wedding band from Papa?" Emma asked as she pulled the ring off her finger and handed it to her mother. "It was in a wooden box of our family things that Miss Robertson had saved from the train wreck."

"Oh, my word! It is! I packed a small wooden box with our important papers and photographs for our move…and I added my ring to the box because my hands were swollen because of my pregnancy. I can't believe the box survived the accident!"

"I have the box with us, Mama. The pictures are clear as the day you packed them in the box."

"Oh, thank you, Emma. This means so much to me," Tina whispered as she hugged Emma.

Tina released Emma and looked at the ring again. "This ring has been passed down through the Martin family for generations. I felt so bad losing it as it was supposed to pass to Robby next. Thank you for bringing it back, Emma."

Carsten gave Emma and her mother time to talk but was glad when Emma returned her attention to him.

"Emma, we posed as a married couple on our trip, and I'd like to continue for the rest of our lives. Shall we make our marriage legal now in front of our family?"

"Yes, I'm ready to wed right now," Emma smiled up at Carsten.

"Shall we move over to the church, so I have my book and a marriage certificate for your ceremony?" Pastor Reagan asked.

"Patrick, you know the wedding ceremony by heart, and I just happen to have a marriage certificate with me," Kaitlyn Reagan pulled the folded paper out of her reticule and held it up for everyone to see.

"Is it already filled out with Emma's and Carsten's names on it? You pulled that stunt with Molly's and Maggie's impromptu ceremonies," Pastor asked his wife with just a touch of sarcasm.

"A pastor's wife is always prepared to help her spouse and congregation," Kaitlyn replied. "Get them married, Patrick. The Paulson Hotel is preparing their reception as we speak."

"This is normal in Clear Creek? Quick weddings and receptions?" Simon asked as he looked around at the crowd.

"The Peashooter Society and the Young Pistol Ladies are *always* prepared," Emma answered Simon dramatically.

"The *who*?" Simon asked as he looked around at all the nodding women in the group.

"Watch out, Simon. The Peashooters and Pistols will plan your future next," Emma said as she pointed a finger at her brother.

"Amen, Simon. Be ready.

"Now, Carsten and Emma, ready to state your wedding vows and become legal?" Pastor Reagan asked as he spread his arms and motioned for everyone to gather around Emma and himself.

"Yes, we are, sir," Carsten said as he moved to stand next to Emma.

She pulled a deep breath from her scented peony bouquet, then smiled and agreed. "I believed you when you said everything would work out for us, Carsten. It's time to make our marriage valid."

Carsten laughed because everyone they'd encountered on this trip believed they were already married. Carsten and Emma worked together as a couple as they faced sadness, surprises, and tragedies. He was ready for their marriage to be real, forever.

The End

~*~*~*~

Give my Word,

Book 3 in series

Here's the description and the first chapter of *Give my Word,* the next book in the Rancher's Word Series.

A sweet historical romance set in the 1890s.

Rancher Beckett Brenner was thrilled to change his destination to escort Greta Wilerson to Kentucky instead of continuing on the planned train trip to Texas.

Beckett, his brothers Asher, and Carsten, along with their neighbors, female cousins, Greta, Alva, and Emma, were on a trip paid for by their respective grandfathers, to explore the women's family's past in Texas' cattle drive history.

On the first leg of their train trip, Greta read in a newspaper the Kentucky Derby was going to be held that very Saturday, and she was determined to be there in person to watch it. Beckett jumped at the chance to escort Greta and they left the group to travel on by themselves.

Hilda, Greta's mother, was a horse trainer first, a wife second, and a mother third. Greta's upbringing meant she was an excellent horsewoman, but also a wild and compulsive tomboy. She wore Beckett's patience thin before they even arrived at Churchill Downs.

But Beckett and Greta work together when they find a scared horse and two injured people in the horse's Churchill Downs stable stall.

Instead of falling in love with each other though, Beckett and Greta find new partners and passions while dodging danger *and* participating in the race of a lifetime.

Give my Word, Chapter 1

"Come on! Come on, come on, *come on*, Beckett! I want to see the horses!"

Beckett Brenner sighed as Greta Wilerson excitedly pulled on his jacket sleeve as they neared the stables of the Churchill Downs racetrack.

He'd readily agreed to accompany Greta to Louisville, Kentucky when the woman declared to her cousins and his brothers that she would attend the Kentucky Derby instead of continuing on their planned trip to Texas.

Three days ago, Beckett and his brothers, Asher, and Carsten, and the neighboring first cousins, Emma Hamner, Greta Wilerson, and Alva Wilerson, were on the train on the first leg of their trip to Texas.

The trip was planned by their grandfathers, Isaac Connely and Oskar Hamner. The young women's grandfather, Mr. Hamner, wanted them to see the Texas Ferguson Ranch where the Hamner family emigrated from Sweden and then started their Texas cattle trail drives up to the Kansas railyards.

His grandfather, Isaac, suggested that the brothers accompany the women for their safety and decide if they wanted to commit to ranching the family's Cross C Ranch for their career. Still, Beckett thought it was a matchmaking scheme.

And it was a *scheme* all right, planned by Greta, to see Kentucky thoroughbreds and the big race in Louisville this Saturday instead of traveling with the group on to Texas.

And Asher and Alva, who were matched in their interests and temperament, left the group, too, to visit the Chicago World's Fair. It was a bold move for his quiet, older triplet brother to suggest he'd accompany Alva to Chicago after she read about it in the newspaper as they sat together on the first leg of their train journey. Asher had secretly liked Alva for years but hadn't gotten up the nerve to court her. Beckett hoped this trip resulted in a match between the two shy and intellectual friends.

Beckett had asked Alva's cousin, Emma Hamner, to a dance last year, but he had no feeling of love toward her. Then he realized that Carsten did have feelings toward Emma, and Beckett didn't ask her out again. Like Greta and Alva, she was another childhood friend with whom he'd gone to the country school and church.

Beckett and Greta grew up together in the ranching community around Clear Creek, Kansas. They'd always been friends, but Beckett was starting to feel used, not thinking of a better word for it.

Greta was enthusiastic to the point that Beckett was feeling exhausted being with her every waking moment. He'd relished the night hours when they were in different sleeping compartments on the train, even though she'd thump the ceiling above her bed to wake him up with a question since he was above her in the top sleeping bunk.

Beckett had enjoyed the change of scenery, traveling through Kansas, Missouri, Illinois, Indiana, and finally arriving in Kentucky. He'd never travelled out of state, and it was an eye-opening experience, not only in the topography but meeting people with different subtle dialects and jobs. Being a rancher, he was fascinated with the other farming communities. Even the color and shape of the barns on the farmsteads varied as the train crossed the states.

"Greta…" Beckett groaned when Greta let go of his sleeve and grabbed his hand to get a better grip on him. "I'm not sure we should be tromping through the stables. You wouldn't like it if a stranger walked into your barn to see your horses."

"That man we talked to back at the entrance said it was all right," Greta protested.

"After you *lied* to him that I was one of the horse's trainers."

"You *are* a horse trainer. I might have implied it was for a horse *here* instead of back in Kansas," Greta shrugged as she walked on to the first barn in sight.

Beckett was interested in getting an up-close look at the horses stabled at Churchill Downs, but he still didn't think they should be back here without the proper invitation.

They both turned to the right at the screams of a distressed horse. It sounded like it came from the end of the building they were near, and the horse continued to shriek its displeasure.

"Greta!" Beckett called out as Greta let go of his hand and ran around the corner of the stable. Becket took off after her, worried the woman would be injured in her haste to reach the horse, which was upset or in pain.

Beckett rounded the corner to see a bay filly trying to break away from a man holding her halter rope in one hand and trying to hit the horse with a Billy club in the other.

"NO!" Greta screamed as she launched herself on the back of the man and tugged on his neck, trying to pull him down. Beckett sucked in his breath, panicking as both the man and the horse continued to fight with Greta in the fray. She was going to get hit with the club or a hoof at any second!

"Hey! What are you doing?" A man called out as he and others ran toward the noise from the other end of the barn. The man trying to hurt the horse dropped the rope, pushed Greta off his back, and took off running around the building.

Greta jumped up and grabbed the halter rope as the horse started to back up into her stall. The horse's shrill voice echoed in the air as she jerked her head around, still upset at the man's mistreatment.

Beckett stopped in his tracks as Greta's Swedish singing immediately caught the horse's attention. The horse's ears changed from flat back against her head to forward to hear Greta's voice.

Greta continued to sing as she slowly moved forward to let the filly sniff her hand and then run it down the neck of the shivering animal. Slowly the horse relaxed and lowered her head at Greta's touch.

"You must know that horse since she calmed down for you, lady. You with Stein's horse farm?" one of the men who came running asked.

"Um, yes, we are," Beckett said to come to the aid of Greta as she continued to stroke the horse's neck.

"Don't know where Stein and his jockey, Will, are, but I'm sure he'll be glad you saved his horse," added another bystander.

"Do you know the man who was trying to take or hurt the horse?" Beckett asked, wanting to tell Mr. Stein what had happened when they met him. Beckett was sure Greta wouldn't leave the horse until his caregivers came back. That's just the way Greta was with animals in general, especially horses.

"Nope, I didn't recognize him, but we'll be on the lookout. He was up to no good," the first man shook his head before turning around to leave.

That was an understatement, but Beckett didn't add any more comment since he didn't know anyone in the crowd, let alone the horse Greta was singing to.

Beckett watched as Greta lead the horse around in circles in front of the stable stall door. The horse kept trying to peek in the door each round but want to go back inside. Was someone else in her stall?

"I'm going to check her stall before you lead her back in, Greta. Something is still spooking her."

Beckett slowly moved to the door's edge, prepared to jump back if there was another intruder caught inside and ready to bolt out of the stall. Even if he didn't have a gun or a club like the other attacker, a pitchfork could be deadly to Beckett.

"There's blood on the horse's hip, but it doesn't seem to be hers," Greta announced as she continued to inspect the animal.

A moan coming from inside the door of the stall made Beckett carefully peek inside the stall. Were these more attackers, or were these the owner and the jockey that maybe the horse was trying to protect?

Two men laid together, one behind the other as if the larger man was trying to protect the smaller person. Both faces had fresh blood on them, and the smaller man's arm was at an old angle, either broken or dislocated from his shoulder.

"Keep the horse outside, Greta. There are injured people in here!" Beckett warned Greta as he knelt beside the men.

The smaller person moaned again, clearly in pain as he tried to shift his position. Becket pulled the first man away from the second since he was unconscious or dead. He had to help the man who was waking up and in agony. Becket gently felt the skinny arm from the wrist to the shoulder and deduced that the shoulder was out of place instead of broken, but he wasn't sure since there was blood on the man's shirt too. The shoulder injury happened to him once when he'd been thrown from a horse. Doctor Pansy Reagan held him down and popped his shoulder back in place. It hurt like the dickens before and during the yank, but it felt better after the shoulder was in place.

Beckett yanked open the man's vest and shirt to see what was bleeding before he pulled the shoulder into place and stopped quickly, throwing up his hands in surprise.

The person had black short-cropped hair on his head, but *she* had her chest bound to conceal her breasts.

Beckett tore open the sleeve next to find the source of the blood, but it wasn't coming from her body, but probably from the unconscious man who had tried to protect her.

"Forgive me, lady, but I need to get your shoulder in place," Beckett murmured as he braced one hand against her upper chest and jerked her arm straight forward with his other hand.

The woman's dark brown eyes opened for a few seconds as she tried to speak through the pain. Beckett leaned closer to try to hear what she was trying to say.

"Please don't reveal my secret. I have to…"

She had to do *what*? And why? Becket didn't know because the woman's head rolled to the side as she passed out.

Please look for Give my Word to continue reading the Rancher's Word series.

Dear Reader:

I hope you enjoyed reading *Believe my Word.* Please help other readers discover my books by either recommending them to family and friends by word of mouth or writing a review. I'd appreciate it.

For more information on this series, you can go to www.LindaHubalek.com, or go online to your favorite retailer, or ask your local library to order them for you. These are standalone stories, but I recommend reading the books in order to get the full benefit of the storyline.

Please sign up for my newsletter at www.LindaHubalek.com to receive a free short story, and to read about the release of future books.

Many thanks from the Kansas prairie!

Linda K. Hubalek

About the Author

Linda Hubalek has written over fifty books about strong women and honorable men, with a touch of humor, despair, and drama woven into the stories. The setting for all the series is the Kansas prairie which Linda enjoys daily, whether by being outside or looking at it through her office window.

Her romance series include *Brides with Grit, Grooms with Honor, Mismatched Mail-Order Brides, and* the *Rancher's Word.* Linda's historical fiction series, based on her ancestors' pioneer lives include *Butter in the Well, Trail of Thread,* and *Planting Dreams.*

When not writing, Linda is reading (usually with dark chocolate within reach), gardening (channeling her college degree in Horticulture), or traveling with her husband to explore the world.

Linda loves to hear from her readers, so visit her website (www.LindaHubalek.com) to contact her or browse the site to read about her books

www.ingramcontent.com/pod-product-compliance
Ingram Content Group UK Ltd.
Pitfield, Milton Keynes, MK11 3LW, UK
UKHW041955190726
13854UKWH00005B/1979